❧ The Hole in the Wall ❧

Also by Lisa Rowe Fraustino

Picture Books

The Hickory Chair

Novels

Ash

Grass and Sky

I Walk in Dread:
The Diary of Deliverance Trembley,
Witness to the Salem Witch Trials

Anthologies

Don't Cramp My Style:
Stories About That Time of the Month

Dirty Laundry:
Stories About Family Secrets

Soul Searching:
Thirteen Stories About Faith and Belief

∽ The Hole in the Wall ∽

Lisa Rowe Fraustino

The characters and events in this book are fictitious. Any similarity to real persons, living or dead, is coincidental and not intended by the author.

(800) 520-6455
www.milkweed.org

Published 2010 by Milkweed Editions
Cover design by Brad Norr Design
Cover photo by Phil Morely, iStockphoto; Peter Zelei, iStockphoto
Author photo by Nick Lacy
Interior design by Connie Kuhnz
The text of this book is set in Rotis Serif by BookMobile Design and Publishing Services.
10 11 12 13 14 5 4 3 2 1
First Hardcover Edition

Manufactured in Altona, Manitoba, Canada in October 2010
by Friesens Corporation, Job # 58711

Please turn to the back of this book for a list of the sustaining funders of Milkweed Editions.

Library of Congress Cataloging-in-Publication Data

Fraustino, Lisa Rowe.
The Hole in the Wall / Lisa Rowe Fraustino. – 1st ed.
p. cm.
Summary: An imaginative eleven-year-old named Sebby discovers that the strange things he has been seing are real, and connected somehow with the strip-mining operation that has destroyed his town, but getting help from his bickering family seems unlikely.
ISBN 978-1-57131-696-7 (hardcover : alk. paper) –
ISBN 978-1-57131-821-3 (e-book)
[1. Supernatural–Fiction. 2. Family life–Fiction. 3. Mines and mineral resources–Fiction. 4. Soil pollution–Fiction. 5. Brothers and sisters–Fiction.
6. Twins–Fiction.] I. Title.
PZ7.F8655Hol 2010
[Fic]–dc22

2010017732

This book is printed on acid-free paper.

for my son,
Dan

“Does the flap of a butterfly’s wings in Brazil
set off a tornado in Texas?”

—*Edward Lorenz*

The Hole in the Wall

Prologue

When he got the idea that would change his life, the boy was lying on his back in the cave near his home. He was staring up with his eyes crossed and waiting for the stone colors to show themselves again.

Months ago he had seen them for the first time. He was playing with his toy soldiers, and as he twisted his head to survey the dramatic battlefield, the colors blinked at the edges of his vision. When he tried to look straight at the bursts of color, they disappeared. It was maddening. He wanted to see them again.

Day after day he returned to the cave, hoping to glimpse the colors. He found that when he read there and his mind was involved in the world of the book, the colors sometimes flickered in the corner of one eye. If he stayed perfectly still at that moment, the colors would linger briefly, bright and pulsing in beautiful shapes that looked like ferns, or maps, or fields of broccoli.

One day he fell asleep in the cave, and as he awoke, before he remembered where he was, he thought he saw the colors everywhere in the walls, every color imaginable, swirling in three dimensions, making patterns like his mother's crocheted blankets. He thought he saw threads of color crocheted down to the middle of the earth.

After that he found he could best call up the colors when he let his eyes float out of focus and turned his mind to daydreams.

Today his mind wandered to a story he'd just read about dragons, and he imagined himself inside a dragon's lair, trying to rob its hoard of jewels while the beast slept. As he reached for a ruby that had fallen away from the pile, the bold colors whirled in the rock overhead like wings flapping. For an instant he thought he could hear something—a musical ringing. The air suddenly smelled sweet.

"Beautiful," he said in awe, though nobody else was near. He sometimes allowed a neighbor friend to join him in the cave, but only to play games or read joke books. He never told his friend about the colors he saw and his friend never saw them. That was his secret pleasure.

And now they were gone again, the dragon's wings buried in lumpy gray stone. The colors always disappeared as soon as he became aware of them, and he was never able to revive the same vision. Each sighting felt like a gift and a loss at once. If he could only make the colors stay longer and hold their beautiful shapes.

While he lay wishing he could conjure up the dragon again, he decided that the next time he'd try to get the memory down on paper, perhaps make a painting. But where could he ever find colors like that? None of his pencils, markers, or paints would be the same. The colors in the rocks had depth, dimension, and motion. How could he capture that spirit on a flat sheet of paper with his schoolboy art supplies?

And then he realized. The colors existed in the rocks. Well, he could get them out! Yes, he'd chip away some stone exactly where the dragon wings had flapped, and he'd grind it down to find the pigments. Surely he could figure out how to turn the pigments into paint.

The boy ran straight home to find a chisel.

❧ 1 ❧

The first strange thing I noticed that cloudy Thursday morning was my brother's cat jumping up on me like a dog when I opened the henhouse door to feed the chickens before school. A cat acting like a dog wasn't the strange part. He's always done that. Which is one reason Pa started calling him Jed's Stupid Cat instead of the name on his collar—Fluffy Kitty.

Stupid had been missing since Jed ran away from home. Back in the fall. I was surprised to see the old furball, but that wasn't the strange part either. Pa had never allowed the cat inside the house. He came and went as he pleased, sometimes disappearing for weeks or months. But this time Stupid had reappeared inside the henhouse. *In*side?! *That* was strange.

Unless . . . did this mean Jed had returned? Excitedly I ran out to the miniature stone castle in our backyard and flung open the door, calling Jed's name. But his room remained as he'd left it six months ago: neatly made bed without him in it, neat piles of books on the floor making a shelf for his neat piles of clothes, guitar under the bed, space heater under the single window. A dozen cuckoo birds stared forlornly from the collection of clocks covering the walls, their weights resting on the floor with nobody to reset them every eight days.

Just then Ma's clunker SUV chirruped outside. She left real early for work at the dress factory in Exton. That's why her chickens were my chores now. Jed used to take care of them.

Suddenly I remembered something. Ma was supposed to sign my homework! I started running down the driveway waving my arms behind the car, but then I ran back to the henhouse before she saw me. Because I suddenly remembered something else. I'd actually sort of forgotten to do my homework. Which happens a lot. Which is the reason Ms. Byron asked me yesterday to get it signed. Ms. Byron was going to have my wild rumpus in detention if I went to school without that math again.

For about the gazillionth time I wished Jed hadn't run away. Jed used to help me with homework.

As I tossed feed to Barney the rooster and his harem, I planned a desperate plea to my grandmother. Grum just had to let me stay home from school, because . . . because I was the victim of a mysterious debilitating illness! Hadn't I grown thin lately even though I ate everything Ma served, no matter how overcooked or underdelicious? Now that I thought about it, I ached all over. My stomach ached, my head ached, my insides ached teeth to toes. Little twitching pains crawled sincerely all along my skeletal system.

I screamed in horror, collapsed and rolled in agony on the straw, then lost consciousness as the ambulance sirens approached. I awoke alone in a hospital bed, my lungs grabbing desperately for air. With possibly my last breath in this life, I croaked, "Nurse!"

The nurse came flying in, crying, "Cock-a-doodle-doo!"

Whoops. There went my brain making things up. Again. Barney was flapping his wings at me while I reached under a chicken for an egg. And that was when I noticed the second strange thing in the henhouse that morning.

The bird didn't move. It sat very still like Grum in church, only its eyes followed my hand as I stole its baby. This was not very henlike. In fact, so *not* henlike that it creeped me out, and the egg fell out of my hand in shock. My shock, I mean. I dove to catch it before it went SPLAT! but only caught the floor with my face.

Instead of going SPLAT! like a decent egg should, the freak went BUMP! and wobbled off like it was hard-boiled. Okay, was my unique brain imagining things again? Always a concern. I smacked myself in the head to check. My head hurt, and when I kicked the egg it didn't crack. This was real.

Not good. Every penny counted around our place, and the first things to go when the egg dollars didn't come in were the fun things. Like Saturday roller skating at the Skate Away.

This situation wasn't natural. It needed attention. With the hard egg in hand, I ran to the house and jumpkicked the door open. The door didn't like to open unless you gave it a good kick or yank, depending on which side you were on. Just one of the many warps in our house A.O.—After Odum Research Corporation bought up all of Kokadjo Gore to strip-mine it. Our place was practically falling apart from soaking up runoff from across the street. Sometimes I swear the water ran uphill just so it could get into our basement. Really!

"Shish! Grum! Look!" Shish is what I very affectionately call my twin sister Barbara, short for Shish Kebarb.

"Oh, shush yourself," she said. She was born seventeen minutes before me but always acted like it was seventeen years. Everything I could do, she could do first. She'd always been taller than me—taller than everyone in our grade, actually. Her eyes were darker brown than mine. Even her feet were bigger. But my hair was blonder and curlier and *that* drove her insane with jealousy. As opposed to just driving her insane.

"What's gotten into you kids, raising your voices like that?" Grum rolled her eyes toward the ceiling, warning us. The cobwebs dangling from the light fan were vibrating with Pa's snores. Pa snored like a jackhammer. It was never a good sign when he stopped jackhammering before 9 AM.

Jed used to say that one good reason Ma raised hens was so we'd always have plenty of eggshells to walk on around Pa.

"But, Grum!" (That was me.)

"Drink the rest of your milk, Barbara Arleene Daniels," Grum added.

A few years ago Grum had broken both of her wrists carrying too many plastic grocery bags. The doctor said it happened because she had bone loss due to osteoporosis. Ever since then she was a lunatic about everyone getting enough calcium and Vitamin D.

"I got an emergency here!" (Me again.)

"Aw, Grum, I hate milk when it's all warm." Barbie can make hate sound sweet.

"Drink it all when it's still cold, Missy, and you won't have that problem. Don't drink it now and you'll have worse problems when you're old like me. You'll be Miss Now-I-Walk-with-a-Cane-and-Should-Have-Drunk-My-Milk-When-I-Had-the-Chance of the Universe. Young women have to put bones in the bank. And sit up straight while you're at it. Slouching leads to—"

This could go on forever. "But the chickens!" I yelled, stomping my feet.

Grum peered at me in her sneaky way, eyes snooping above her glasses as she looked up from the snarled ball of string that she untangled hour after hour because she liked to keep her hands busy, and, "Waste not, want not." I knew I was in for one of her lessons of the day.

"But the chickens? But the chickens! Is that what passes for a complete thought nowadays? The chickens are a lonely subject in search of a predicate."

"They have a pox! Look!" I held my hand out and dropped the egg.

"Seb!" squealed my perfect sister.

The egg went BUMP! wobble-wobble-wobble and stopped against Grum's slipper. She put her string ball down and made clickety noises with her false teeth as she poked at the egg with her toe.

"Why, it's like a rock! I've never seen anything like it. Were there others?"

I made a face and shrugged. I didn't recall encountering any other eggs in the hospital.

"Well, pick that egg up for me, please, then go back out and finish your chores. While you're at it, send up a prayer for Jesus to lift the burdens from those hens." She started humming a hymn, and I was out of there.

I used to love every minute with Grum, when she had her own place across the road in Kokadjo Gore and I could visit her whenever I wanted. But after she moved in with us it was too much of a good thing. Worst of all, she took the room I used to share with Jed, so I had to move into the upstairs foyer with Barbie. Jed moved into the stone playhouse us guys had built in the backyard. That was back in the days when Pa got up at 6 AM and had a charming personality. When I used to follow him around and "help" him be a fixer-man.

Finishing my chores in the henhouse turned out to be impossible. I kept looking and looking, but I didn't find enough eggs to refill a carton for the Dogstars, our regular Thursday customers. Finally I realized the reason was that the eggs just weren't there. And neither were some of the chickens. They must have gotten out when Jed's Stupid Cat let himself in. I certainly would never have left the door open after all the times Ma reminded me.

I'd have to look for the escaped hens outside, but not now. I barely had enough time to get ready for school.

As I ate my cereal, I stared at the eggs in the basket, wondering if they were hard like the one that went BUMP. I didn't dare try the drop test, for obvious reasons. While I was staring, my arm started aching again with those twitching pains along the bones. I screamed and grabbed my elbow.

"Oh, puh-leeze, Sebby. Cut the melodrama. Just give me your dirty rotten dish so I can wash it before we miss the bus." It was Barbie pulling on my cereal bowl, which was still attached to my arm.

Grum hushed us again and said, "Your sister's right, boy."

I moaned sincerely to prove my pain. It hardly had anything to do with the fact that I didn't have my homework. Signed. "But, Grum, I honestly don't feel good. I ache all over. Even in my teeth."

"That so?"

I nodded.

"Well, open your mouth and say *ah*."

I did a real good job of that while Grum shone a flashlight down my throat. "Hm, I wonder . . ." She stuck a finger in my mouth and probed my gums in the back.

"Ow!" (She'd definitely hit a sore spot.) "Ow! Ow! Ow! See? I'm in agony, Grum. I can't possibly go to school today."

She removed her finger, put down the flashlight, and pronounced, "You're getting your twelve-year-molars is all. You'll be fine. Congratulations." She patted my cheek.

"What? That can't be! We're only eleven!" Barbie grabbed the flashlight and ran into the bathroom to look for molars in the mirror.

Ha! It killed her that I'd finally gotten ahead of her at something. But this was no time to gloat. I still had a mission. "Grum, what about the rest of my aching body?"

She lifted her head and eyed me under her glasses this time, stopping at my ankles with an *Aha!* smile. They stuck out under my frayed jeans like white bed knobs beneath a short bedspread.

"You're an inch taller today than yesterday. They're just growing pains. Now go change into your school clothes, young man."

But it was too late for that. The Rust Bus already sat at the end of our driveway, flashers blinking. I grabbed my bag and raced Barbie for the good seat.

2

B.O., or Before Odum took over Kokadjo Gore, a regular big yellow school bus used to take us to school with a bunch of kids from there. Now that all those families had moved, we rode in a rusty blue Ford Escort with a yellow sign in the back window that said SCHOOL CHILDREN ABOARD. The driver lady, Miss Rosalie, worked as a cashier at WalMart and picked us up in her own car on her way to and from work.

"Hey, now, Sebastian, quit mauling your sister and let her in the car," Miss Rosalie greeted me fondly. "You rode shotgun yesterday. Plunk yourself down back there in the middle to save room for Cluster. And fasten your seatbelt."

So I gave Barbie a shove into the good seat and grumbled my way into the back next to the car seat that held Miss Rosalie's drooling baby. He grinned and bonked me on the head with his rattle.

Little Rico wasn't the problem with the back, though. I sat next to him gladly on the way home in the afternoon. The problem was the ugly view out the window on the left side of the car when we drove across Kettle Ridge in the morning. From that high up, the strip mine looked like a skeleton with scabs and tumors. The graveled backbone road was nicknamed "The Gash" because that's what it looked like in the scarred land. Rib roads ran down between slag piles and stagnant water holes.

One time Jed brought home some girl he'd met at a rally for

peace or the environment or the protection of animals or something. She asked us what strangers to these parts always ask: "Kokadjo *Gore*? What kind of a name is that?" And Grum answered as always: "A gore is a triangular piece of land that got left out somehow when the towns around here were surveyed, back in the Colonial Days."

From Kettle Ridge you could actually see the triangle shape, like a giant wedge had been cut into the earth. The ridge rose straight up at the widest end, with the stripped land gradually narrowing to a tip a couple of miles away. The Gash cut across the wedge diagonally from near our house to the center of town. If you knew where to look, you could make out a camouflaged bump in the middle of the triangle. That was the ORC compound.

The sight of Odum's triangle of wasteland made a crappy start to the school day. Much better to look out the right side where ORC hadn't turned nature into an ashtray. Off to the right, the land looked the way the gore used to—rolling hills with big old trees and boulders wherever the land hadn't been cleared for gardens or homes. Pretty. Lots of wildlife. Turkeys had often wandered through Grum's backyard with their heads bobbing. They made me laugh. And Pa did, too, when he used to take me and Jed trout fishing in the brook out behind Grum's, telling us the adventures he and little Stanley Odum had while growing up in the gore.

No fish in that brook now.

As soon as I strapped myself in next to Rico, I knocked three times on Barbie's head. "Hello, can I borrow a pencil?"

"Quit it! Only if you aren't going to ask me to forge Ma's signature."

"I can't believe you'd even think that. Can I borrow your math?"

"Do your own math."

"What if I pay you?"

"You don't have anything I want."

Oh, didn't I! Wouldn't she love to know about my hideout, the Hole in the Wall. Barbie would have to give me her math and sign Ma's signature every day for a year to make it worth sharing my best secret with her. I went there every chance I could sneak away from the house.

"You know the deal," she said. "You give me your shoe, I give you my pencil." This was so I'd remember to give her the pencil back. Usually when I stepped in a mud puddle. Which was often. We got a lot of rain in Kokadjo.

"Aw, c'mon, do I have to?"

"You'd lose your own belly button if it wasn't tucked in. Your shoe or no pencil."

No choice. I threw my holey sneaker into her lap.

As Barbie dug for a pencil I leaned over Rico and let him pull on my curls so I could watch for Cluster Dogstar to emerge from the woods on the right. It was better than looking the other way and getting all depressed.

Cluster Dogstar, the new kid in eighth grade, was the only one besides me and Barbie who rode the Rust Bus. Her parents used to homeschool her until Cluster crossed her arms and said, "I'm never going to read another word or multiply another number or speak to you ever again unless you put me in a school with other kids, and you can't make me change my mind." Then she clamped her lips shut and waited for September. On her first day of school she discovered computers, and she didn't want to go home.

The Dogstars all had weird names. Blue Moon was Cluster's unexpected baby brother, Marigold was her mother, and Goldenrod was her father. Marigold had changed her name from Mary Jane, and Goldenrod had changed his name from Rodney, but Cluster and Blue Moon were the kids' real names.

Cluster walked like a deer, picking her steps carefully. Which made her more fun to watch than doing fractions. Maybe she just did that because the path she walked had actually been made by deer. There wasn't a driveway to her house. I'd never been inside, but everyone knew that the log cabin where the Dogstars lived didn't have electricity or indoor plumbing. At least I had a television to watch, even if Pa hogged it, and I could brush my teeth over the sink when Grum wasn't in the bathroom. Sebastian wasn't a great name, but it wasn't Blue Moon.

"Peace, my friends." Here she was, floating into the Rust Bus like an apple blossom in the wind. Cluster always talked like a grown-up flower child, and she always seemed to be floating like some kind of petal.

"My goodness, Sebastian, you are looking upright this morning," Cluster said.

"Yeah, it must be all that cold milk I drink," I said. "What's new with you?"

"We already had a visitor at the Love Shack this morning." Cluster called their house the Love Shack. People in town called their place Zensylvania or just "the commune." Pa called them whacked-out yippie-hippie-doo-da-dopeheads and told me and Barbie to stay away from there.

I hoped the visitor was someone interesting. Like the longhair with sandals who had started hiking from British Columbia to join the commune thirty years ago and just showed up last August. For the most part, though, more people left than arrived at Zensylvania (especially A.O., After Odum). Now it was pretty much down to the Dogstars, that longhair guy, and a bunch of goats.

Not surprisingly, Cluster said, "A representative from Odum Research Corporation came to test our water again."

The Dogstars got their water from a pure spring, and they bottled and sold their Zenwater to health food stores. Last fall, their dog Red Dwarf had suddenly gotten sick and died. The veterinarian said the cause was something Red Dwarf ate or drank. Cluster's parents went to town and knocked on Mr. Stanley Odum's door. Nobody except them knew what was said, but the next day Cluster told us some of Odum's goons showed up to put a fancy water purification system into their spring. (Well, she actually said some "representatives" showed up. At our house, we called those people "Odum's Goons.")

While they were at it, the goons brought one for our well too.

"Wasn't that generous of my old buddy Stan to give us that high falutin' H_2O gadget for free?" said Pa. Like most people in town, he gushed over Stanley Odum like he was some kind of hero when he opened up the Stanley T. Odum Zoo and the Boys of Summer Stadium.

"So generous that he doesn't want us to get sick off his polluted runoff and sue him," Jed said.

Those two had a difference of opinion over everything. If Pa said sneakers, Jed said sandals. If Jed said blue, Pa said red. And arguments over Odum could go on for hours.

"Of course Stan doesn't want us to sue him," Pa said. "He doesn't want *anyone* to sue him, ergo he does the right thing. That's how the free market is supposed to work. It's the American way."

"Yep," Jed said, "that's the Corporate States of American way, all right. Put your childhood buddy out of business and then refuse him a job as a lousy janitor in your stinking rich company. Good guy, that Odum."

Jed was talking about the time Pa went to apply for a maintenance job at ORC and couldn't get past the front gate because he flunked the employment test. Actually he couldn't even take the test because it was digital. And Pa wasn't.

"Teenagers. You think you know it all when you have no idea what you're talking about. Stan's not a bad guy. He'd have hired me if he could. It's not his fault I don't know how to use all that technocrapola he's got over there."

"There is such a thing as retraining, Pa. Education. If your generous benefactor didn't see fit to provide that for all the schmucks who did things the old-fashioned way before he took over the town, then at least you could get yourself back to school and learn how to function in the world we're actually living in today."

With arguments like that overflowing in our little house, I didn't know what to think about Odum. Good guy, bad guy, which was he?

"Oh, Mr. Odum is neither one nor the other. He's human. He's both good and bad."

I snapped my head toward the voice beside me. Cluster Dogstar in the Rust Bus. Yikes, had I been talking out loud? I thought I was just thinking to myself! Or had Cluster read my mind? I wouldn't put that past her. I snapped my head the other direction to look for clues on Rico's face. He had his toe in his mouth.

"So how did the water test turn out?" I asked Cluster.

She shrugged. "They just took a sample. We'll find out the results later today."

"Do you think there's a reason they keep checking? Something they know is wrong?" Jed would think that.

"I really can't say."

What was that supposed to mean? Did Cluster not know, or

did she know something she wasn't allowed to tell? I'd have asked her if she didn't already have one leg out the door. By now we had reached the Mildew School, and the only thing Cluster had on her mind was going online.

The Mildew School was my name for our branch of the Stanley T. Odum Education Center because of the way it turned gray no matter how often they repainted. The superintendent said the problem kept recurring because the building was situated over a high water table in the valley and had big shade trees growing around it. But I didn't remember the school ever being gray before the strip mine. Everything in town turned gray no matter what. When it was wet, the mildew grew. When it was dry, the dust settled. Gray, gray, gray. Pa said everyone should just paint everything gray and stop whining about it.

I hopped to sixth grade homeroom on one foot pretending I was a stork, then quickly finished scribbling my math so I could get my sneaker back. I even felt pretty good about a couple of the answers. Not Ms. Byron. She shook her head sadly as she handed my page back, with a tiny red zero in the corner like a swatted gnat. I wondered if giving bad grades hurt Ms. Byron more than it hurt us.

"Sebastian, you're obviously having some trouble with numbers. You did page 127 instead of 238. How about you and I stay after school and get you caught up?"

The class thought that was very funny. But Grum says there's always a bright side, and there was. At least now I had a good excuse to walk home. It was only a mile if I cut across the gore, and I could go straight to the Hole in the Wall instead of having to slip through the clutches of Grum and Pa. They always had their own ideas about how I should spend my time.

That afternoon after doing page 238 (and 230, and all the

pages in between) I zipped down the block to the IGA on Main Street. Behind the garbage dumpsters out back a big old tree had broken during an ice storm and left a branch leaning over the tall fence that surrounded the gore. That branch was how I got in A.O. on the town side. On the home side, I slipped between two gigantic boulders they hadn't crammed together closely enough to stop me and my bike.

You wouldn't use either the front or the back gates if you wanted to sneak around ORC, since both were guarded by goons with guns. The roads all had lampposts with surveillance cameras on top looking around like birds of prey, and they broadcast menacing *caw-caw-caw* noises to keep real birds from nesting there.

To me those caws translated to a challenge: "Dare you to sneak by! Dare! Dare!" How could I resist? Besides, I was getting bored snooping around Zensylvania. The most exciting thing I'd ever seen there was Marigold hanging diapers on the clothesline. No, wait, it was when I climbed one of their trees in the winter and could see in our kitchen window. I caught Grum waltzing with a mop.

Poking around inside the gore wasn't anything like looking down on it from Kettle Ridge. It was still disgusting, in concept, but being in the middle of it was also very, very interesting. After two years of sneaking I knew the gore inside out. Well, everything that wasn't inside the Onion, anyway. The inner compound was a lichen-green dome half buried in the middle of the triangle like a gigantic overripe onion. If you looked down on it from a plane, it would blend in with the ground so you wouldn't even know it was there. To find it you'd have to practically bump into it, like I did the first year of the mining.

It had been a cold day in November, before the first snow.

One second I was combing for rocks, and the next second I was staring through an electric fence that seemed to pop up out of nowhere. A big barking blur of black was coming at me. It was a hungry Doberman, and there were more where he came from. If not for the fence I'd have been Kibbles 'n Bits. Luckily my surge of terror adrenaline got me out of there before the goons could catch me.

After that I went back and found a slag pile where I could spy from a distance without getting the Dobermans stirred up from their underground kennels. Mornings when I didn't have school I borrowed Grum's binoculars and hid there. I saw how the goons scanned their hands in front of an electric eye to make the gate open, and then how they disappeared into a tunnel that led to some underground parking area. The compound had to be huge under there. I watched bulldozers, backhoes, and dump trucks go back and forth day after day, bringing big rock chunks back to the compound and hauling loads of dirt and gravel back out.

Why did they pulverize all those rocks? It really bothered me. Because I liked rocks. Loved rocks. I even collected ones that looked like something—a heart, a frog, the state of Maine. Called them my art rocks. What was ORC mining that they had to ruin all those rocks? And why hide their big secret underground?

I was dying to get inside that place and find out, so I decided it would be a good idea to make friends with the Dobermans. Maybe they'd let me sneak inside through their kennels. They were very skinny, and I thought they'd love to have some home cooking, even if it was Ma's. But my plan had to wait for winter to end so I wouldn't leave footprints in the snow.

The first spring night after a big thaw, I sneaked the left-overs out of the fridge and took them as close to the electric fence as I dared. We'd had hockey puckburgers for dinner. I flung them over the top, and sure enough, the dogs came running. You'd think they'd pounce on the hamburgers and wag their tails in thanks, but no. They didn't even stop to sniff. They just stood at the fence barking their faces into froth. I knew from one time I'd seen the dogs bark at a lost skunk that a pack of goons would be running up out of the kennels in about ten seconds with guns cocked. I made dust out of there. I was Robin Hood escaping the Sheriff of Nottingham, just running without thinking of where I was going, scrambling up and down piles of slag.

And that was how I stumbled onto my secret place. Tripped over a tree root and when I stopped doing somersaults, I found myself looking up into a maple at a squirrel looking down at me. Birds were tweeting like an audience laughing.

Whoa! Trees! Animals! Sherwood Forest! And obviously straight from my imagination, because how could it possibly exist inside the big fat ugly pus-pool Odum had made out of the gore? But I found my way back the next day, and it was still there. A real oasis. *My* oasis. Nobody else in the world knew about it. If they did, the ORC goons would've mined the smithereens out of it like they had every other inch of the gore. It was located at the tip end of the triangle and partly hemmed in by slag piles.

At first I just went to my oasis on sunny days and lay in the deep bed of moss in the middle of the trees to read my comics. Sometimes I'd hold my finger up to trace the pattern of my favorite maple up and up, each branch stretching out into other branches almost but not exactly the same. Sometimes I'd draw it. Two squirrels often chased each other along the limbs. It amazed me, the way their fooling around could make the whole tree shiver. They'd skitter off balance, then save themselves by catching hold of a tiny twig as if it were the easiest thing in the world.

The problem was, I couldn't go to the oasis on the days when I wanted to the most—the rainy ones. It drove me bonkers staying in that tight little house with Ma's stinky cigarette smoke and Pa's blaring TV and Grum's ugly tangled yarn blob. Jed had let us hang out in his castle (formerly known as our playhouse), but Barbie was always out there reading and complaining if I breathed too loud.

Then one day while I was picking raspberries from the bushes that grew high at the back of the oasis, I discovered the cave. It was just tall enough to stand in at the center and deep enough to sleep in. Like a six-man tent. Roomier than my so-called room at home, a lot more private, and just as comfortable, too, by the time I got done remodeling.

First I made walls out of stones at the outside edges of the cave, fitting each rock just right, like Pa had taught me when we made the play castle. He could do any kind of handyman stuff, but masonry was his best thing. Ma kept a photo album of the rock walls and fireplaces he'd built in the gore. Now the pictures were the only things left of them.

Next I found a piece of warped plywood in Pa's scrap heap and rigged it up as a drawbridge. Then I dug a moat around the entrance and lined it with clay to catch water and drain into the little brook that bubbled up from a spring nearby. Near where we used to fish. I liked to imagine we were back there, me and Jed and Pa.

Inside the cave I made shelves out of rocks and boards. I brought over some blankets, snacks, comics, and some of my rock collection (not the little pebbles I liked to hold in my hand to help me stop thinking at night and fall asleep).

It took me weeks, but when I was done I had myself a little palace. The Hole in the Wall.

After math detention that Thursday when strange things started happening in the henhouse, I saw another strange thing at my oasis. The water bubbling up from the spring was all colorful and foamy. Not a pretty sight. Well, the colors might have been pretty in a rainbow, say, or on a T-shirt. In spring water, not so much. I sure hoped the squirrels weren't drinking it.

I grabbed a handful of raisins from the stash I kept inside and munched on them while I read my comics. The raisins had dried out so much I couldn't chew them with my sore twelve-year-molars, so I just swallowed them whole. Normally I would have washed them down with a swig from the spring, but not today. That rainbow water scared me.

∽ 3 ∽

You'd think when a kid gets home from a long day of school torture, the first thing he should hear is, "Hiyuh! I missed ya! How was your day? Want some milk and cookies?" No. I get, "Hey, you boy. Didn't you see the lawn mower?"

Yeah, Pa. I almost tripped over it on the way in. It was parked in front of the doorstep. Give me a break. I just walked five miles up and down Kettle Ridge for all you know, and now you expect me to mow those little tufts of moss poking out of the mud? The green stuff that grew in our yard A.O. couldn't rightly be called a lawn, but we'd been having warm weather for March and whatever the green stuff was, it was growing.

"Can't I at least have a snack first?" Without waiting for an answer I grabbed a handful of stale Oreos from the cupboard.

"Have some of Odum's M&M's," the Shish called from upstairs. Where I'm sure she was already doing her homework.

Har-de-har-har. Odum's M&M's were the mold and mildew that crept up from the basement into all our walls, floors, and ceilings ever since the strip mining began in the gore. The winding gray curlicue patterns the stains left would have been kind of cool if you didn't know what caused them. The basement of this old house had already been a little tilty, but now it seemed to be sinking like it was built on quicksand instead of solid rock. Every wall in the house had huge cracks, the tile had come off the bathroom floor, and the grout pulled away from the edges of the sink and bathtub so often that Ma just kept the grout squirter behind the toilet with the plunger and the scrub brush. During one long wet spell, mold even formed on coats hanging in the closet.

"It's a wonder mold doesn't grow on Pa," was another thing Jed used to say.

No sooner had I stuffed the last Oreo in my cheek and started to mow the lawn than a pang of pain went through my toe. I'd stepped on a sharp rock again, right where my bones had worn through the bottoms of my sneakers. If Ma had a penny for every time she worried about money, she wouldn't have anything to worry about. I'd decided to wait until my toes poked through the front to let her notice I needed new sneakers. Being broke rotted.

As if that weren't bad enough, after the next step I took, the lawn mower went ZZZZING and conked out. "Worthless rocky land!" Which I learned from Pa. He used to swear all the time at those *blankety-blank* machine bustin' rocks until one day he gave up trying to roto-till a garden plot for Ma and instead started digging up every fieldstone in sight. He laid them all out in the yard like a jigsaw puzzle to see what he could make out of them, and I helped. When we were done a few weeks later, we had our play castle and a smooth mowing lawn. Until the runoff from ORC started churning up rocks from China.

Back in the present, Pa's voice came at me from the door: "Hey, youngster, I don't hear any grass hitting the dust." As I yanked the cord to restart the mower, I muttered all the curses I could think of and repeated the best ones.

The machine gave my hands a prickly feeling that wiggled all the way to my nose and ears. It brought back the aches and pains I'd suffered in the morning, only worse. I was in a hurry to finish and end the pain, so I didn't even notice when the glossy black pickup truck with extralarge wheels pulled into the driveway. I only noticed it after I'd turned around and stopped short to avoid mowing a pair of pointy cowboy boots. Real leather. You could almost smell it mixed in with the mud and cut grass.

There was only one person who wore boots like that: none other than Mr. Stanley Odum. Behind his back some people even called him "Boots" because he wore the pointiest, clickety-clackiest, leatheriest cowboy boots on earth. People said you could smell those boots coming before you could hear them, and that was about three minutes before you could actually see them.

What was Boots Odum doing at our house? That made four strange things in one day. The sun was low and glaring right at me. I squinted to get a good look at him. I'd never seen him up close and personal before. I'd been spying on his secret compound the day he came around to taste our ultraviolet purified well water.

Boots Odum was on the tall side and husky up top, with a jean shirt straining the buttons over his belly. But skinny down bottom. His pants rode low with nothing to hold them up.

I'd have recognized his face anywhere, since it's plastered all over the billboards for the Boys of Summer Stadium. It would've been a plain face if it weren't for his big round nose planted in the middle like one of Grum's dahlia bulbs. Average brown eyes. Hair military short on the sides but long on top—probably combed across a bald spot. Plain mouth. Smooth-shaven face, no dimples, crags, or clefts. A couple of crow's feet around the eyes. Not counting the boots and pickup, the guy didn't look rich or powerful or like a rocket scientist.

Then he grinned and became a walking billboard. Odum's big warm smile lit up the whole front yard. Rich. Powerful. No question about it.

It had to be those teeth. Big, straight, shiny white teeth with just a little bit of a gap between the front two.

Stanley Odum was what Grum called "a Self-Made Man." Like Pa, he had graduated from Kokadjo Prep, which was what Kokadjo Gore families used to call the public high school, owing to the fact they didn't pay taxes and had to pay tuition. Unlike Pa, Boots went off to Exton City to work his way through college and graduate school. Then he got himself a fancy job in some faraway place. Pa said he was some kind of rocket scientist for the government. He discovered and invented things. Nobody knew exactly what he'd discovered or invented, but whatever it was had made him rich. Whenever he came home to visit, he quietly bought up land in the gore, making cash deals with the owners. Including Grum. She used the money to pay for her new dentures, bought the clunker that Ma's driving now (which was an upgrade), and put the rest away for Jed's college. Well, Barbie's, too, and possibly mine, if I make it through sixth grade.

Finally, when Boots Odum owned it all, he moved back home to start ORC.

Jed had a joke: "Why did Stanley Odum start wearing cowboy boots? So he could pull himself up by his own bootstraps!"

I cut the motor to the lawn mower and waved a little hello to Boots Odum. He lifted his right hand and waved a little hello back with two fingers that fluttered faster than a movie starlet's eyelashes. Nice trick!

"Hey there, buddy!" Pa's voice boomed from the doorway. "What brings Kokadjo's finest citizen by our humble abode today?"

"That." Boots Odum pointed to Ma's sign, written on cardboard with a marker and stapled to an oak tree by the road.

FRESH EGGS
4 SALE
$1.50 DOLLARS/DOZ

"Thought I might try my eggs fresh from the hen for a change. Only a buck fifty! A good buy."

And a good-bye to you, too, I almost said, but instead I bit my tongue and said "Ouch." Odum gave me a puzzled look as he reached into his pocket and tugged out a fat wallet. No wonder his pants rode so low. He shuffled through dozens of Ben Franklins and Ulysses S. Grants and a few Andrew Jacksons before he pulled out an Abe Lincoln.

Pa reached into his pocket for his wallet. Which was very skinny. Odum held up his hand. "No problem, Craig—keep the change. If you ask me, Claire doesn't charge enough for her hard work. Fresh organic eggs ought to be at least twice the price of those mass produced at a factory farm."

Yeah, whatever he said!

"A dozen eggs, comin' atcha," said Pa, "laid fresh this morning," and he disappeared inside.

Odum made a squinty face at me. "Can't see too good without my glasses, son," he said, pulling a pair out of his shirt pocket. The lenses were milky colored like seashells. Eerie. My neck prickled with goose bumps. Then Odum smiled, and the glasses fit perfectly with those pearly whites.

He started wandering around the yard, sidestepping the mud, kicking a rock now and then. He picked up a pebble and tossed it from hand to hand, whistling "The Star Spangled Banner," when Pa threw open the kitchen window to call in the charming polite voice he used in front of anyone not related to him, "Sebastian, could you please come in here for a moment?"

Who, me? Usually I only answer to "Hey, Seb, get your *blankety-blank* in here." But since we had company I went along with it.

"Stan, we'll have the freshest eggs in the world ready for you in a jiffy," Pa said with a nod and a smile.

Inside, Pa was on his knees in front of the refrigerator. Jam jars, juice cartons, Cheez Whiz, mustard, leftovers, and all sorts of stuff was spewed all over the floor.

"Where the blazes are the eggs for sale?" he said.

If there weren't any cartons on the special shelf just for eggs, we didn't have any for sale. Ma had explained it time and again. I looked at the front door, wishing her and Grum would choose this second to walk through it. Why did it have to be Senior Citizen's Discount Day at Love Your Hair? Why did Grum even need her hair permed? It always looked like asbestos anyway.

"We must be sold out," I said. "Except for those." I pointed at the basket of eggs on the counter next to the sink, waiting for Ma to wash and carton them for the Dogstars. She was very particular about that part of the business and didn't want anyone else doing it.

Pa put his forehead in his hand and rubbed the wrinkles. Then he looked up at me again with that watch-out edge in his eyes. "I promised the man his eggs. Why didn't you tell me they weren't ready? Are you ever gonna get your head out of your rear, boy?"

With Pa there's no use answering questions like that. No matter what you say, you just get yourself into more trouble. The only hope is to get him on another track.

"Bet you anything Ma kept some eggs out for us to use. We can give them to Mr. Odum. They're still fresher than store-bought. He'll never know the difference." This, I decided, would be safer than suggesting that Pa wash and carton the morning eggs himself.

"Ain't no eggs in this refrigerator! Can't you see I've looked!"

After all these years finding room for his beer in the fridge, you'd think he'd know where we keep our own eggs separate from the ones for sale. I'd have fished them out myself, but I wanted to stay out of arm's reach from Pa.

"Try that veggie compartment," I said, pointing. "Sometimes they're in there." (Always.)

He pulled out a cardboard egg carton like a rabbit out of a hat, then tugged up his belt loops. Pulling himself together.

"Aren't you going to count them?" I said.

Pa glared at me, fumbled with the carton notches, then let loose a curse that made even my ears burn. "Eleven!" He looked around wildly at all the walls, as if to find one more egg behind the calendar.

I hurried to the sink, carefully washed the crusted slime off a fresh egg so I wouldn't break it, dried it on my T-shirt, and handed it to him.

Pa grunted. "Well, you know where everything goes. How about cleaning up this mess for me." That was as close to a thank you as he ever got. He readjusted his belt loops and took the carton out to Boots Odum. I hurried out and pretended to adjust the lawn mower gizmos so I wouldn't miss anything.

Our new customer was holding Jed's Stupid Cat, rubbing his chin in fur while Stupid tried to lick him all over the face. I don't know what surprised me more—that Odum liked cats, or that Jed's cat liked Odum. Some watchdog.

"Sorry to keep you waiting on your eggs," Pa told Odum, "but when you put in a fresh order it takes a few minutes for the hens to lay 'em."

Odum put the cat down to accept the egg carton. "Thank you muchly."

"So, enjoy!" Grin.

"I intend to!" Grin. Odum squealed out of the driveway. His megawheels spit gravel behind him.

Pa let Boots Odum go without even asking him to bring the carton back when he returned for more eggs. Ma always asked. She lived by a motto, "Use it up, wear it out, make it do!" Even when Pa was bringing in money, she'd take us clothes shopping at thrift shops. Nothing made Ma more excited than paying one dollar for a brand name that looked like new.

I was wondering if the thrift shop at our church had sneakers when Shish yelled out the door, "Sebby, Pa said to get in here right this second and do what he told you."

Where had she disappeared to in the middle of all that egg business? She had a way of doing that. Now you see her, now you don't. But she was always there to boss me around. Like magic. With a perfect fingernail pointing at me.

"What? I can't hear you!" I yelled as I yanked the lawn mower cord. I knew she'd clean up the mess. She loves to keep the peace as much as she loves doing her homework. And her nails.

When I put the lawn mower away in the storage lean-to behind the house, Jed's Stupid Cat was there with his head in a bowl of milk. "Putting bones in the bank, eh, fuzzball?" I said, rubbing his head. He made figure eights around my ankles. I was glad someone had thought to feed him.

After supper there was a knock at the door. "That's probably the Dogstars on their date night," said Ma from her sewing machine. She had decided to take in some of Jed's pants for me so I could cover my ankles.

Yeah, good old Marigold and Goldenrod thought it was real romantic when they left Cluster to babysit and strolled hand-in-hand down the road to get their fresh organic eggs every Thursday. They traded with Ma for goat cheese. Which tastes better than it sounds. I grabbed the carton Ma had ready and jumped up to get the door, leaving Spiderman alone to cast his webs around the prepositions on my English worksheet. The page was looking pretty magnificent, if I do say so, but I'd been toiling over it for five whole minutes and needed a break.

It wasn't the Mr. & Mrs. at the door, though. It was Cluster, seeming to float like a water lily even with chubby little Blue Moon strapped onto her back, asleep. And that was the fifth strange thing of the day. She'd never come to our house before.

"Why, hello, you must be Cluster," said Ma. "How lovely to meet you. Come on in." Ma flashed me her don't-be-rude look, and I realized I was blocking the way. I moved aside. Cluster floated into the kitchen.

"Wanna play with us?" piped Barbie from the TV tray where she sat playing rummy with Grum.

"Do you have any computer games?" Cluster said, looking wistfully toward the crappy old Commodore 64 in the corner. Jed had bought it and kept it going. Now when we turned it on, the screen just said READY followed by a blinking block. And that was all.

"Not at the moment," I said.

Pa muted the TV and sat up, buttoning his shirt. "How are your fine parents this fine evening, young lady? I hope they aren't indisposed healthwise." The four empty beer cans that just a moment ago had decorated the coffee table had now magically disappeared. Pa seemed quite the fine fellow. Like someone who would never dream of calling anyone's parents whacked-out yippie-hippie-doo-da-dopeheads his kids should stay away from.

"Marigold and Goldenrod are well disposed," said Cluster, handing me the goat cheese in a recycled tofu container. "Thank you for asking. They sent Blue Moon and myself for the eggs because they're . . . busy."

"Busy doing what?" I said. It didn't occur to me that I shouldn't have, until all eyes in the room laser beamed holes in my head. The mouths opened to spit fire at me too. I threw up my hands and yelled, "Sheesh, sorry!"

At that Blue Moon woke up and howled. Cluster forgave me with a nod, gave her regrets to Barbie on the card game, and took off like dandelion fluff in a high wind. We heard Blue Moon until his wails faded with distance.

"What do you suppose is ailing that baby?" said Grum. "It couldn't be colic, could it? His mother is so careful about her diet."

"Don't you mean about *his* diet?" Pa said.

"No, Marigold breast-feeds," Ma said. Pa turned red and cranked up the TV volume.

"The baby must be teething, then," said Grum.

"Like Sebby," Barbie threw in, getting quite the laugh out of all except the one person who was glaring. Which was me.

I know this may seem entirely coincidental, but at that very moment a bunch of little knives stabbed inside my stomach. It was all I could do not to wail like Blue Moon.

"You think it's funny to have four toothaches and all kinds of growing pains and a bunch of little knives stabbing in your stomach?" I doubled over with the cramps and started to cry.

That was proof of my sincere misery. I can't fake cry, and to be honest I would never even want to.

Ma got up from the sewing machine and came running to my side. She soothed me and forced the pink chalk medicine down my throat and tucked me in to bed. To help me sleep I held a pebble in my hand next to my cheek, the smooth greenish oval with dark specks that I'd found on the beach once when the whole family went camping at Lake Exton—fishing, swimming, playing Crazy Eights half the night under the gas lantern with bugs flying around it. Those were days to remember.

൙ 4 ൙

Friday morning instead of her typical "Up'n at 'em, Seb, chickens waiting, don't forget to close the doors," Ma's first words to me were, "Honey, are you all right? Do you need to stay home in bed today? Grum will nurse you."

When she put it that way, the aches and pains in my body hardly made me want to wail at all. I could live with them. Because my chances of having an okay day were way better out of bed than in it with Grum on guard and Pa in control of the remote. He watches too many horror movies. Besides, I just remembered I'd never hunted down those chickens that Jed's Stupid Cat had let out. Ma would kill me surer than my mysterious debilitating illness if she did my chores and found out how I'd slacked off.

If it hadn't been pouring rain I would have hunted down every last chicken that morning. I did glance around the yard as I ran to the henhouse, but I didn't see any signs of hens on the loose. Barney and his harem were in the same state as the day before, and I found barely a dozen eggs.

At breakfast Grum said I'd grown another inch since yesterday and no wonder I felt so achy. Barbie stood back-to-back with me to compare heights, then turned around and glared. I'd caught up with her!

"Don't worry, Shish, you'll always have browner eyes and better grades than me," I said. "And longer fingernails. What does it matter if I get taller?"

"I haven't grown one bit since we got our school clothes this year, Seb. I don't care if you're taller than I am. *I* want to be taller than I am!" At that she ran up the stairs crying.

"Your sister has growing pains too," Grum said, nodding wisely.

Now that I thought about it, half the girls and a few of the boys in sixth grade had outgrown Barbie this year. Now she was just average. Did being tall mean that much to her? Now I felt bad for her, but I didn't know what to say, so I ate more cereal.

Ma sent a note to school about my not feeling too good last night, so Ms. Byron didn't keep me after for detention even though I forgot to get my homework signed and Spiderman didn't get it finished. Plus, he circled *is* as a preposition. When *is* actually isn't. It's a verb, according to Ms. Byron, even though it doesn't show action. I guess she must know. Anyway, she was a little disappointed in me.

My teachers always act surprised when I do bad in English. They think I'm supposed to be some kind of verbal genius from the way I talk and draw stories and use my imagination. And apparently I actually scored high on some test once. Which I don't remember taking. Back in first grade the teacher told Ma that I was "gifted and talented," just like Barbie. Ma told Pa, and he said, "Don't let that genius malarkey go to your head, son. If you can use your hands you'll be better off." I believed him then, my wonderful Pa who could build a castle in the yard. But now that things had changed, I wondered if maybe he was wrong. Maybe I ought to put my mind to learning why *is* is a verb even though it's so lazy.

I thought about all that on the Rust Bus ride home. While ducking Rico's rattle and digging little shreds of yellow foam out of the ripped seat. Barbie didn't want to talk; she was busy doing her math. I didn't have a pencil, but I wouldn't have done any schoolwork anyway. It was Friday afternoon for crying out loud. I would rather spend the time talking to Cluster, but she'd stayed home from school.

"Maybe the baby is sick with something contagious, and Cluster came down with it too," Barbie had suggested that morning after Miss Rosalie gave up waiting for her to float out of the woods. We waited a long time because it was unthinkable that Cluster would miss school. She hated weekends and vacations—they kept her off the Internet.

Too bad Cluster was indisposed healthwise that day. I wanted to find out the results of the tests Odum's goons did on the Zenwater.

Normally when I kicked my way in the front door of our house and the musty smell hit me in the face, it felt like I'd just lost a fight. But that day an unbelievable sweet smell greeted us when Barbie and I got off the Rust Bus. It smelled so beautiful I could hardly stand it, like being stuck behind the Perfume Lady in church. Every time she sits in front of us it makes the sermon seem twice as long. Grum says she must be hiding something.

Friday was Ma's early day home from the dress factory. She looked up from the bills spread out on the table and said something about my clothes. I don't know what, because I was intent on looking around for the smell so beautiful it could drown out Odum's M&M's and Ma's cigarette smoke.

Barbie leaned over to look in the oven window. "Ooo! Cookies! What kind are they? They look like swirling rainbows."

"Homemade cookies!" Usually we got the expired store brand cookies on clearance sale. "I love you, Ma!" I was overcome with feeling. Homemade cookies could mean only one thing—dough in the refrigerator! I loved raw cookie dough almost as much as art rocks. I pushed past Barbie to get at it. A big blob of dough went straight in my mouth and another fingerload was on its way when Barbie shut the door on my arm.

"Sebby!" said Ma, Grum, and Barbie in unison. "No eating dough."

"I know, I know, raw eggs can kill me," I said, chewing. Man, that dough tasted like heaven.

"I don't care about that, but your dirty hands will kill us," said Barbie.

"Seb, go wash up, please, and put on those pants of Jed's I took in for you," Ma said. "You and Barbie are going to bike into town and deliver eggs to Boots Odum, and you need to look presentable. Can you believe that man? All these years he's never bought a single egg from us, and now all of a sudden he wants dozens, two days in a row. And delivered by the kids! What does he think we are, Domino's Pizza? I told him delivery's five dollars a dozen, *five!* And he didn't even hesitate!"

From the living room couch came the sound of a throat clearing. I looked Pa's way and saw the keep-your-big-mouth-shut look in his eyes. No wonder Ma seemed surprised that Odum thought her eggs were worth so much. Pa must have pocketed Odum's tip yesterday without telling her!

"Do I have to go? Can't you just drive Barbie to do it? Me and Spiderman were really hoping to get our homework done." (Really we planned to spend the rest of the daylight out at the Hole in the Wall. Without prepositions. Or verbs.)

Grum looked up from her rat ball. "That's 'Spiderman and *I,*' subject of the verb, and don't be a lazy boy. Why should your mother waste gas when you have two good legs? By the way, did you ever tell her about that bad egg?"

"What bad egg?" Ma choked, trying to talk to us and exhale

her smoke out the window at the same time. She's always trying to quit, and when she's not quitting she tries to keep us from breathing her second-hand smoke. But I figure if I can smell it I'm breathing it, and I even smell it upstairs in my bunk when she smokes in the basement. Our whole house is a smoker.

"Cigarettes cost more than eggs," I said. I don't know where that came from, but I had to do something quick to get the how-dare-you look off Ma's face. "What I mean is, maybe Mr. Odum is willing to pay the price because it's fair. Fresh organic eggs ought to be at least twice the price of those mass produced at a factory farm, if you ask me."

Pa growled for attention. "Nobody asked you that, boy. Are those real ears on your head, or are they just painted on? Your mother wants to know about some bad egg."

"Oh, right." I'd forgotten that. "Yeah, Ma, there's something wrong with the chickens. They've been laying funny—half the usual amount, today and yesterday, and one was just like a rock. One egg, I mean. I put it in the plant pot so it wouldn't get mixed up with the others." I didn't tell her that the diminished amount problem might possibly be due to escaped chickens. (Oh yeah, which I planned to look for at the first available opportunity.)

Ma frowned hard, ground out her cigarette butt in her smiling-mouth ashtray, put her hand on her forehead, and stared at the bills on the table. Then she slowly got up and went to pluck the egg out of the plant pot.

"Barbie," she said absently, staring at the egg, weighing it in her hand, "I want you to do the talking when you deliver the eggs. Sebby, you be polite, now, you hear me?"

"Are you sure you want to give Mr. Odum any more eggs?" said Barbie. "I mean, what if there's something wrong with them?"

"You wouldn't want Boots breaking one of his big shiny teeth on an omelet," I said.

Ma sighed and tapped the rock egg on the counter. Thump, thump, thump. It didn't even crack. "He was quite insistent that he wanted eggs laid fresh this morning. They ought to be all right. This bad egg is heavier than normal, really dense. The eggs I used in the cookies seemed perfectly fine."

Another idea occurred to me, and it was a Grum-pleaser involving the use of my two legs. "Hey, Ma," I said in my most reasonable voice, "Barbie doesn't even have to come. She can stay home and help you, and I can—"

"Yep, just painted on for sure, those ears," piped Pa. "You'd better start listening to your mother, or else I'll change your channel." He pointed the remote control at me like a gun. Then he laughed.

I closed my eyes and counted to ten and tried to think a happy thought about Pa to calm my thumping heart down, like Ma's always telling me to do. I thought about how I used to follow him everywhere and he'd let me spread the mortar between rocks or hammer in the stake when we set up the tent. But that just made me miss the old Pa. All I wanted to do now was run at the Pa we had now and pound that smirk off his face. Instead I slammed out the door, grabbed my bike, and took a running start up the hill to Kettle Ridge.

Stupid hill. Stupid Shish. She was slowpoking her way after me. If I'd been going alone I could have cut through the gore to town. I'd have saved half an hour each way, to say nothing of both lungs. And had time to spare at the Hole in the Wall.

Kokadjo meant "kettle" in Abenaki Indian, and that's exactly what the mountain looked like, an upside down kettle. After you got to the top, you'd ride straight across for a stretch, and then you'd coast down the other side of the kettle to Main Street, Kokadjo. But before coasting, I always stopped at the top to catch my breath. And tried to make myself look to the right, across to the distant mountain ridges and foothills packed with trees and jutting rocks, rolling down into a valley checkered with stubble fields. Oh, but like driving by an accident scene, there was something irresistible about the horror. I always had to turn my neck and stare at the gore.

Somewhere at the bottom of the jaggedly torn cliff that used to be the next mountain stood my little oasis, the Hole in the Wall, but you couldn't see it from here. I tried to spot it every time, but it was way back near the V end of the wedge shape, hidden behind slag piles. I was glad nobody could see it, or that might be the end of it. Off on the right side of the gray land skeleton, the town of Kokadjo made a little green nick in the edge of the strip mine. Just like the lip of a dirty ashtray.

That afternoon on my way to Boots Odum's house, staring at his gore mess made my stomach lurch, like a bowling ball was knocking pins around in there. I bent over with pain. Suddenly my teeth were killing again too. And my leg bones. Stupid growing pains. Had Jed gone through this? Man, I wished we could talk about it. He always knew how to make me feel better, and laugh while he was at it.

Barbie was still far behind, zigzagging up the steep slope using the lowest gears on her bike. She hates sweating. I didn't feel like waiting to hear her whine. Soon I was way ahead of her on the long coast to town. That gave me extra time to pop wheelies in the Skate Away parking lot. Which helped me forget my miseries. By the time I remembered to watch for Barbie again she was a block away from Odum's mansion, and I had to pump the pedals to catch up.

Since the house was so fancy I used my kickstand and

made my bike use good posture instead of flopping it on the sidewalk.

The place went on forever with porches and cupolas and wings and twists and turns. The front door alone was as big as our kitchen wall. My feet couldn't resist poking around in the pretty rock gardens. The guy had some major art rocks holding in his daffodils. One looked like a gray rabbit sniffing the air. Another looked like a fox curled around its kit. They looked so real, I thought I saw one move.

"Wow, get a load of that door knocker," I said. It looked like a lion's head. I ran up ahead of Barbie onto the stone porch while she pried the egg carton out of her bike rack. I stuck my fingers in the lion's mouth and knocked his mane about thirteen times. It sounded so cool.

"Sebby, cut that out. You're embarrassing me." She was combing her hair, straightening her clothes, and scowling like I was roadkill. "Back off from the door," she said. "Your breath could drop a yak. You don't want to give Boots Odum a rude impression when you say hello."

"I don't give a cheese doodle what anyone thinks of me," I said as the giant door started to swing open.

ꕥ 5 ꕥ

I expected to see the walking billboard behind the door, but instead we faced a plump lady around Grum's age, dressed in a faded housecoat and scruffy slippers, with silver hair cut shorter than mine. Which I couldn't help but notice since her head seemed to point straight at me, poking out of her shoulders like a turtle's. Her back was hunched way more than Grum's. She had the absolute worst case of Not-Enough-Milk-When-I-Was-Your-Age Disease I'd ever seen.

At that moment I decided to love milk and sit up straight forever.

At first I assumed the woman was the housekeeper, but then she twisted her head sideways to get a look at us, and her nose looked just like a dahlia bulb planted in the middle of her face. That woman could only be the mother of Boots Odum.

Her face lit up. "Children!" she said. "Why, I was just telling my Stanley this morning at breakfast how much I miss seeing children. There used to be so many of them running around the gore, coming to visit me. I know they really just came for the candy, but I loved talking to them all the same. I'm Mrs. Odum, by the way. Call me Miss Beverly—the kids in the old neighborhood always did."

"Uh, candy?" I said.

"Would you like some?" Miss Beverly said. "I'm sure I have goodies left from Halloween, and candy canes from Christmas.

Come on in and let me find you a treat. But first you must tell me your names."

"I'm Sebby and she's the—"

"I'm Barb," the Shish said quickly, glaring at me out of one side of her face while the other smiled sweetly at Miss Beverly. How did she do that?

"Thank you, Miss Beverly, but we really shouldn't impose on you," Barbie said. "We just came over to deliver these eggs to Mr. Odum." She held the carton out. "And if it's not too much trouble, my mother would like the carton back next time you want a refill."

"Eggs? Oh, yes, Stanley had quite the sparkle in his eyes when he told me someone would be dropping by with them. Someone! That trickster! He knew you children were coming to make my day! Well, hurry in so we won't heat the outdoors. The money's in the kitchen." She took the carton and shooed us inside.

The first thing I saw was myself in a hall mirror. Holy oops. I'd taken off without changing my clothes. My old jeans were frayed at the bottom from when they used to drag on the ground, but now my bed-knob ankles stuck out over my mismatched socks. Grass stains floated like green clouds above the knees. I'd always been kind of husky, but now I looked skinny, except across the shoulders. My T-shirt stretched tight on top. And it was on inside out. I didn't have to sniff to know I was carrying half the chicken coop around on my grubby sneakers. The last time I combed my hair was before church last Sunday. No wonder Barbie was so embarrassed by me.

"You have a beautiful home," Barbie said, and then I turned to take it all in. The room was all gussied up with antique furniture, paintings, statues, flowers. The floor was the glossiest wood I'd ever seen. Curtains, velvet. They looked like wine.

"It's nice enough," said Mrs. Odum, wincing, "but it's hard to keep clean. Stanley pitches in when he can. He wants to hire a cleaning lady, but I told him I know how to keep house, thank you. People don't belong anywhere they can't take care of their own messes, that's what I say."

"Cleaning is hard work," Barbie said sympathetically. "We do a lot of that at our house, too."

"Miss Beverly, you got any . . . M&M's?" I said, poking the Shish in the ribs.

"Why, Sebby, I just might!" Miss Beverly said.

"Will you please shut up?" Barbie whispered with an elbow back at me. Wow, she'd definitely gotten shorter. She stuck me in the arm instead of the head.

All the way to the kitchen Miss Beverly described the treats she might have hidden away, but I wasn't paying attention. I was too in awe of the sights on the walls. The artwork was amazing. Paintings of ferns and broccoli and waterfalls, shells and Queen Anne's lace and trees, all from different angles that showed the little details you usually never notice. Every nook and cranny held a sculpture. Even the antique furniture looked like it ought to be in a museum.

Barbie stepped on the back of my sneaker when I stopped to stare at the humongous painting at the top of the staircase. It showed a planet from outer space. The landforms looked like Earth, but it wasn't your typical big blue marble. Beautiful patterns of color swirled down from the coastlines, meeting in the middle in whirls of lava. Somehow the artist had made the flat canvas seem like a magical globe, like you could reach inside the painting all the way to China. The water moved with the tides; the lava looked molten.

"You like that painting?" said Miss Beverly proudly. "My son gave it to me for Christmas. He used some newfangled paint he's working on to make spacecraft stronger. *Land of the Adri* is the title, whatever that means. He tried to explain, but I didn't understand. Too many fancy words. That one is called *Fractal*." She gestured toward the broccoli we'd just passed.

Or was it broccoli? From this angle it looked like the coastline on a map. One minute it was a head of broccoli, the next it was the world.

The next painting looked like one of the sketches I'd drawn of the maple branches at the Hole in the Wall. Only Odum's was way better. I had a lump in my throat so big I couldn't breathe. I always get this embarrassing lump when I see something beautiful. One time when I went to a museum on a class trip, I walked around with a lump in my throat all day, hoping nobody could see it from the outside. Looking at the art in Boots Odum's house, I thought I'd suffocate.

Miss Beverly smacked me on the back to help me catch my breath. "Thank you," I said. "Those paintings rock."

"They certainly do," Miss Beverly said with a smile. "I'm sorry about all this dust and cat hair." She sounded discouraged. "Come along, we'll fix you up with a glass of lemonade."

She did seem the type to have twenty-seven cats, and on the way to the kitchen, I looked around for them. I didn't see any cats, but I did see a few hairballs caught on chair legs.

Meanwhile, Miss Beverly kept talking. "I tell Stanley he should start an art gallery, he's so talented, but he says he's too busy with his engineering. It keeps him going day and night, that corporation. Lucky he never got married and had kids. They'd never see him! He's a workaholic." She made it sound like a compliment, though. I wondered what it would be like having a workaholic for a father.

The kitchen was a huge, sunny room. Miss Beverly made us sit at the wooden table while she bustled about, pouring glasses of lemonade and pulling candy out of cupboards. In the middle of the table a fruit bowl sat heaped with big, shiny apples that you just knew were crunchy instead of squishy. Juicy green seedless grapes, which we hadn't had for weeks because they were too expensive in the winter. And huge, fat oranges like I'd never had in my life, the kind you buy one at a time. We always got the mesh bags of skinny faded oranges.

And then there was the pebble. At first I thought I'd imagined it. While I salivated over the oranges, I could swear I saw colors flashing somewhere near the fruit bowl. Like those occasional flashes of color in the slag piles that drove me so mad. When I looked straight at the colors next to the fruit bowl, though, all I saw was a plain gray pebble. It could have been any pebble from the brook at my oasis.

I picked it up and held it to the light of the chandelier, hoping something would happen.

It did. Something incredible! The colors returned, every color imaginable, blinking in swirling shapes that seemed to reach out toward me. In an instant I was surrounded by gorgeous colors and shapes like one of Odum's paintings. Sounds like wind chimes filled my head. For some reason I thought of the foaming colors yesterday in the brook near the Hole in the Wall.

Then, suddenly, an alien with three gigantic nostrils and five enormous brown eyes appeared before me, saying, "Earth to Sebby."

Barbie peeled my fingers back from what I held.

"A rock! You nerd boy. Leave it to you to forget all about candy and the most delicious fruit in the world at the sight of a boring pebble."

Boring? Couldn't she see what I saw?

"Have an orange, Barbie, if you'd rather. Eureka!" said Miss Beverly, hauling half a bag of M&M's out of a fancy dish.

Barbie set the pebble back where I'd found it. I watched it flit a few more colors at me before going gray.

Man, I felt confused. My brain often takes me places that I like way more than my real life, but I kind of always know I'm playacting. This time I wasn't sure. When I held the rock up to the chandelier, I was really *there* inside those swirling shapes.

A faraway voice said, "Do you like that rock, Sebby?"

Barbie poked my arm, swallowed politely, and said, "Miss Beverly wants to know if you like that rock."

All I could do was nod, but Barbie had plenty to say. "My brother's always bringing rocks home as souvenirs, everywhere we go. He has rocks in his head."

Miss Beverly smiled as if she understood. "Stanley too! You know, he has lots of those lying around. I'm sure he wouldn't miss one little rock. Why don't you keep that one, Sebby?"

"Wow. Do you really mean it?" I was so happy, my grin made my ears ache. Now I wouldn't have to borrow the rock without asking. Which had just crossed my mind.

"Oh, sure, don't worry about it," she said with a casual swipe of her hand. "Stanley is the most generous man in the world. He'd give anyone the shirt off his back."

I was starting to appreciate the side of Boots Odum that hadn't flooded our basement or made Grum steal my bedroom. Happily I reached down the tight neck of my inside-out T-shirt to drop the art rock into my pocket. And I'd just swallowed my first handful of M&M's—the chocolate kind—when the rock started to wiggle around like it was looking for a way out.

For real.

I screamed and flew out of there before Barbie could finish digging her nails into her orange.

The Shish caught up with me at the top of Kettle Ridge. I was staring off toward the Hole in the Wall, wishing I'd gone there instead of to Odum's, catching my breath, and wondering if I'd just gone crazy. Do sane people think rocks can move?

She must have been pumping the pedals hard. She'd worked up a dripping sweat, and I could barely understand her as she huffed and puffed her words. "What's wrong, Seb? Why'd you take off so fast?" She was worried about me.

What could I tell her? The truth was too embarrassing. How could I have ever thought a rock was wiggling around in my pocket? It had felt like it was throbbing against my heart. But any ding-a-ling could figure out that it was really the other way around. I'd never felt so stupid in my life. And a lot of the time I feel pretty stupid.

"I have a stomachache," I said. Which was the truth. But I was trying not to think of that.

"Then why did you grab your *chest* like you were having a coronary before you took off?"

Before I said any more I wanted to see what that weird rock was up to now. During the wild ride, I'd rolled it into my sock to get it off my chest. When I loosened the material, the pebble fell to the asphalt and spun in loops. It made a wind-chime sound that flashed my memory straight back under Miss Beverly's chandelier. Crazy!

As the pebble fell still and silent, I looked to see if Barbie had seen and heard it too. Her bike stood leaning against an oak. She herself had ducked behind the tree. All I could see of her was half her face with one enormous surprised eye. She was scared.

I knelt to pick up the pebble.

"Leave that thing alone, Seb! There's something wrong. It might hurt you."

"Sheesh, take it easy. It's just a rock. Hey, when I was fiddling with it at Miss Beverly's, did you see anything strange?"

"You mean, like, besides you waving that thing around with your eyes crossed?"

"No colors?"

"You mean the colors from the chandelier?"

Oh, right. I hadn't thought of that. The light was made of stained glass. Maybe staring into that had made my eyes go kaleidoscope. Had I imagined the whole thing after all? I wanted to find out.

The sun was an orange ball hanging low over the western hills. I held the pebble up so it was encircled by orange light and flopped it around in a figure eight. Well, I found out, all right. Instantly the pebble went blinky again. In fact, the more I flopped it, the more excited it got, swirling with bright colors in arcs like a butterfly's wings flying toward me, and making that soft wind-chime music. It was so beautiful, I could barely breathe past the lump in my throat.

The next thing I knew, the music in my ears morphed into a wild shriek. *Aaaaargh!* Barbie. She'd come running up behind me to give my hand a hard smack. The rock went flying into the dead oak leaves beside the road and sat there looking gray, forlorn, and kickable.

"Hey!" I said, running to its rescue.

Barbie raced after me and tackled me to the ground. My hand reached the pebble first, and the moment I touched it, the thing started winking colors again. Then Barbie jammed her hand under my arm to tickle me. Me and Barbie probably had our first knock-down drag-out in the womb. She was born knowing all my weak spots. I doubled over groan-laughing, and she grabbed the pebble away. The colors instantly stopped. Jumping up she thrust her arm back as if to throw a shotput, aiming across the road and over the cliff into the gore.

“No! That’s my rock!” I cried, lunging at her knees, taking her down. And we rolled around wrestling, like we’d done so many times before. Except this time, as I pushed on her and she pushed back, I felt like I was the stronger one, like it wasn’t even a fair fight anymore. I knew I ought to quit before she got hurt. But I wanted that rock. It was awesome. It might even contain the secret to what Boots Odum was doing in the gore.

No way could I let my sister throw it over the cliff.

6

On second thought, maybe me having superior strength was just enough to make things even. Barbie was really limber. When I pinned her down by the arms, she flipped her legs up around my waist and rolled me over. So then I pinned her by the legs, and that was even worse. She tickled me weak. Finally I sacrificed my sense of honor and pulled her shirt up. I'm not proud of that, but it got the job done. She let go of me in shock, and I got hold of the pebble long enough to sink it deep into my pants pocket where I knew she would leave it alone.

With her shirt tucked in Barbie hopped to her feet and stood nose-to-nose with me, practically hyperventilating with anger.

"You know that isn't a normal rock, Sebby! Rocks are cold, dead things. That one is *alive*! It's *magic*! And magic's *evil*! You have no business keeping it."

"Come off it, Barbie." I sat on the guardrail to get some space, catch my breath, and put the gore behind me, out of sight. "That rock is just doing whatever comes naturally. There's no such thing as magic. Everything has a scientific reason. We just don't always know what it is." Jed was always saying that.

"Sebby! That rock is scary! It even scared you at first! What if it's radioactive or something? It might cause cancer. You might grow three heads with snakes for hair. Have you thought of that?"

"If it was radioactive, Madame Curie, do you think Boots

would be leaving it next to his fruit bowl? He has a ton of them lying around, his mother even said."

"You'd better pick up your bike before it gets run over, Boots Junior."

"Yeah, go ahead and change the subject just because you're losing," I said, but I must admit that I heard a motor roaring up the hill, and my bike sat in the middle of the road where I'd let it drop when I got off it.

I wheeled it to the curb just as two balding tires smoked to a stop right next to us. And between them, a rusty red pickup door with faded lettering:

CRAIG "JACK OF ALL TRADES" DANIELS
HOME HANDY MAN
CALL FOR THE MOST REASONABLE PRICES ON EARTH!

The window rolled down and Pa's hairy fist spilled over the edge of it, holding a plastic baggie with an egg inside. "I wanna know what's going on, boy."

If my stomach didn't already hurt before, it would now.

"I d-d—I have no clue what you mean, Pa." Had he seen me fighting with Barbie? If so, I was in for it. Pa thinks boys should never hit girls, unless of course they're fathers instilling discipline.

"You know exactly what I mean. I wouldn't put it past you to set up this whole egg thing to get out of your chores in the morning. Slip the chickens some d-CON, maybe? I've heard what a hard time you give your mother when she gets you out of bed, you lazy good-for-nothing kid."

How could he hear that when he was snoring so hard? But I didn't ask. I leaned hard on my bike and looked out over the gore. It was better than looking at Pa's eyes.

"Pa, I didn't do anything to the chickens, I swear!"

"Well, your mother nagged me to drive two hours all the way over to the state university agricultural lab and drop off this petrified egg. They told her on the phone they'd try to figure out what's wrong. If I get over there only to find out you've been pulling one of your tricks, you're gonna wish you were never born!"

I already do. Did I say it, or just think it?

Pa leaned at me. I could almost feel his three-day beard scratching my nose. I held my breath so I wouldn't have to smell his.

"What did you say?"

"I didn't do anything wrong, Pa. I didn't!"

Pa glared and nodded. "We'll see about that, won't we." He thwacked the baggie against my head before he drove off.

As I rubbed the sore spot, the Shish halfway smiled. "Hey, Seb, Pa just left an egg on your head."

I took that as an invitation to make up. "Sorry about . . . you know. I just really wanted my pebble."

"Yeah, I owe you one," she said, and took off coasting downhill to home. It didn't take her long to pay me back, either. The moment we got in the house, she handed Ma the Abe Lincoln Miss Beverly had given her and said, "Mr. Odum's mother is really cool. She gave us candy and fruit and let Sebby bring home a rock that you're not going to believe."

"Isn't that nice," said Ma as she squirted mustard on slices of canned meat. "I hope you didn't spoil your supper, though."

"Sebby, aren't you going to show Ma your pebble?" Barbie smiled smugly my way.

I tried not to smile back. Little did she know.

"Sure," I said, turning out my pockets. Blue balls of lint drifted out, but no rock. Because on my way inside I'd dropped it under the porch. Nobody but me would ever find it. Except for maybe Jed's Stupid Cat, who was sitting under there guarding the house.

"Uh-oh," I said. "I must have lost it on the way home."

Barbie looked disgusted. "Ha, ha, Sebby. You put it somewhere else. You just don't want to show Ma. Cough it up."

I shrugged my most innocent shrug with my palms up. "Why wouldn't I show Ma?"

Ma put her gourmet supper recipe under the broiler, then stood up with hands on hips to face us. "What's so special about this rock that you two are making such a big deal out of it?"

"It's nothing special," I said. "Just a plain old gray pebble. I only took it as a souvenir."

Barbie growled. "Ma, that rock . . . !"

I crossed my fingers and wished she'd keep going. Let her try and explain all about the evil magic rock that made music and light displays. Then who would have the reputation for making up wild stories? This could be entertaining.

Barbie squinted at me, then rolled her eyes. "Oh, never mind." She punched me hard in the arm on her way upstairs to do whatever she does when she gets away from me. *Now* we were even.

After dinner that night, Ma got her homemade cookies out. *There* was something to take my mind off everything else. I held my first one up to the bare light bulb over the table to study it and tried not to think about my aching stomach. The entrée of burned mustard-on-Spam hadn't helped my belly any. I actually left some food on my plate. Ma asked why, I told her, and she gave me a shot of the pink chalk medicine. It helped a little. Enough to slip in dessert.

"I think that I shall never see, a thing as lovely as this cookie," I said with dramatic flair. The cookie was round and pale yellow like the sun, no burned bottom, just the faintest ring of light brown around the edges, hinting at the possibility of a chewy middle.

Enough anticipation. I shoved half the thing in my mouth and chomped down.

The pain! The pain! It shot through my twelve-year-molars and cheeks up into my eyes. That cookie was a rock. "Yow!" I jumped up and ran to the mirror. "Ma, you broke my new teeth!"

In the background I could see Barbie staring strangely at her cookie. Carefully she put an edge in her mouth and nibbled. She nibbled harder. She twisted and gnawed and nothing happened to the perfect cookie. She made a face.

"Is this another one of your so-called jokes about my cooking?" Ma picked up a cookie and took a bite. "Ow!" She put her hand to her mouth and stared at the cookie forlornly. "But I timed them! They aren't burned! What could have—oh!"

She put her head in her hands. "Oh no . . ."

"What's the problem out there?" called Grum from the bathroom.

"Those godforsaken eggs," Ma said. "There's something wrong with them after all. They calcified in the cookies. I sure hope Stan Odum hasn't tried to eat any of them yet!"

No wonder my guts felt like a bowling alley. I'd eaten two great big blobs of that cookie dough! I groaned at the thought of what I was in for. As Grum always says, "What goes in must come out."

"I'm going to have to give his money back and get those eggs off him," Ma was saying. "How on earth am I going to explain?"

If he ate the eggs, Boots Odum might wind up in the same predicament I was in. Ha! "Don't bother," I said. "It's his own fault anyway. He asked for fresh eggs laid this morning, and that's exactly what you gave him."

A killer point, I thought, but Grum called, "Remember the Golden Rule." Then the toilet flushed. It made me laugh, but I guess nobody else got the humor. Ma and Barbie frowned at me.

"What about the Dogstars?" Barbie said. "The eggs they traded yesterday came from the same batch you put in the cookies."

"Dear Lord, that's right!" Ma was pacing now. "I can call Stan Odum and warn him, but the Dogstars don't have a phone. I'll have to tell them in person." She looked out the window and ran a hand through her hair. "But it's already getting dark, and I don't even know the way to their house. Do you kids?"

"We've never been invited," said Barbie, shaking her head no. Um, well, me and Grum's binoculars might have made the acquaintance. But that didn't mean I'd know my way in the dark. I just shrugged.

"Guess I'll have to go first thing in the morning, then," Ma said.

"But what if they have eggs for breakfast before you get there?" Barbie wondered.

That made me remember something. "Cluster wasn't in school today. Maybe she already ate some of those petrified eggs and they made her sick!"

Ma gasped and covered her mouth, making the worry in her eyes stand out. "We'd better go right now. You two come along and help me find the trail."

"Do I have to go?" said Barbie. "I want to finish my homework so I can enjoy the rest of my weekend." Good thing I already had barf medicine in my system. Of course Ma said she could stay home.

Ma grabbed a flashlight and we hopped in the SUV. She parked along the shoulder on the good side of Kettle Ridge, and we found our way to the trail Cluster emerged from every morning. Cluster called it the Trace. It had been made by animals in ancient times, she told us, and Native Americans used to follow it when they migrated. The Trace was well worn, but still not easy to follow on a dark and cloudy night this time of year. The ground all looked the same, covered by dead leaves and pine needles, with no summer growth around the trail yet. Plus it was slippery. Ma kept grabbing my arm and saying, "Watch your step, don't fall."

I didn't say so, but I was a little scared. The woods smelled wet and rotten, like something had died. All around us we could hear rustling and the noises of animals doing their night things. There were bears in these woods, wildcats, possibly rabid foxes, porcupines that could quill us, skunks that could spray us. Our own breathing sounded loud in the deep quiet. It had turned cold, and that made everything seem louder. An owl hooted right over us, making both of us scream and jump and then laugh at ourselves nervously.

We walked about ten or fifteen minutes and then reached a steep hill. From there the woods opened into a valley meadow with a boxy shadow looming at the center, a building with soft lights barely glowing in a couple of the upstairs windows. A trickle of woodsmoke made gray curlicues in the black sky. They reminded me of the mildew stains in our house.

"Welcome to Zensylvania," I said.

"Lovely," Ma said. "Well, let's hurry up and get this over with." And she led the way downhill to the cabin. It had been handmade out of trees on the property. It made an awesome silhouette with logs jutting out at the corners.

"Oh, my goodness! I can't believe this." Ma aimed the

flashlight at a shiny white square on the door. A sign, it looked like. A very familiar sign. You couldn't go a hundred feet around the edges of ORC without seeing one just like it:

AUTHORIZED PERSONNEL ONLY

TRESPASSERS WILL BE PROSECUTED

ARMED PATROL ON DUTY 24 HOURS

VIDEO SURVEILLANCE IN PROGRESS

ODUM RESEARCH CORPORATION

"The Dogstars must have sold out," Ma said in disbelief. "I thought they never would."

I had a sinking feeling about that. "Cluster said the goons came to test the Zenwater yesterday. I bet it flunked." Had it turned all colorful and foamy like the spring at the Hole in the Wall? Suddenly I felt scared for my friend.

"Whether it did or didn't, I don't see how they possibly could have moved out this quickly. And there are lights on upstairs. They must still be here."

Ma poised her hand to knock at the door.

"Wait, Ma!" I shone the flashlight around searching for hidden cameras, but only saw animal eyes glowing from a tree. "Ma, you sure you want to knock? What if the people inside are Authorized Personnel Only?"

"What if they're the Dogstars? I have to warn them about the eggs. Let Stanley Odum try and prosecute me for doing the right thing."

At that, Ma swallowed hard and rapped loudly on the door.

7

We waited, listening for footsteps inside, and heard nothing but the wind in the trees and the roof settling. Bats swooped and rose in chaotic patterns. A puff of wood smoke wafted by, making me cough. Feeling the cold, I blew on my hands and jogged in place.

Ma knocked again. Still nothing. She reached for the doorknob. My heart quickened as her hand twisted.

The latch clicked. The door swung open with a long, spooky squeak. Ma shone her flashlight inside and screamed. My heart stopped. The Dogstars lay on the floor before us, moaning and frothing at the mouth, their skin splotched with colors like in the polluted spring at the Hole in the Wall.

No, my brain made that up. Must be all those horror movies Pa watched on the TV. Ma didn't scream. She still had her hand on the knob. It didn't turn. The door was locked. My heart restarted.

"Maybe they just left a candle burning when they left," she said, turning to look at the pale ribbons of light the upper story windows cast on the yard.

"And a log on the fire," I added.

"Well, nobody's answering the door, so we might as well go," Ma said.

We hurried back along the trail, wondering out loud where our friends had gone so suddenly. "Surely tomorrow there'll be word around town," Ma said. I hoped so. I didn't like not knowing what happened to Cluster.

When we got home I stooped to retrieve my hidden souvenir pebble. It wasn't hard to find—it winked at me when I poked my head under the steps. Nice pebble.

It was past our bedtime, so Ma sent me straight upstairs. Barbie was already in bed reading. At first she didn't sound concerned when I told her everyone at the commune had been abducted by aliens, or else maybe put into the witness protection program, or else maybe buried in a mass grave under a slag pile in the gore.

Barbie just rolled her eyes at me. "Sebby, you're outrageous. Did it occur to you that they just decided to go somewhere? Like, a concert? Or a long weekend vacation?"

Then I remembered to tell her about the ORC sign on the lodge door, and reminded her about the water test, but she was still being stubborn. "Goofball, Boots Odum has been trying to buy Zensylvania out for years. Maybe he just made them an offer they couldn't refuse."

Ma came upstairs and kissed us good night. "Lights out, now. Time to stop talking and go to sleep."

"I second that," Grum called from the bedroom formerly known as mine.

Pa wasn't home yet, so the house was perfectly quiet when the phone rang. Not even a whole ring. Just a chirp. A sound that always made me happy even if it stopped me from getting to sleep.

"Jed!" I blurted.

"Praise the Lord for good news," said Grum.

"Amen," said Ma.

Barbie sighed and jiggled happily in the bottom bunk.

The day after Jed ran off, Ma filed a missing persons report with the police, but they said there wasn't much they could do since he'd turned eighteen. About a month later, he called for the first time. He didn't stay on the phone long and wouldn't answer any questions. He just told Ma how he'd be calling every so often and letting the phone ring once to let us know he was okay, because he didn't want us to worry. Whatever number he called from, it never showed up on Caller ID. We had no clue where he'd gone or whether he'd taken Stupid with him, but we were glad to know he was okay. Well, maybe not all of us. Pa said Jed must have gotten himself into some kind of serious trouble with the law to be sneaking around like that, and we were better off not talking to him. But I believed in my brother.

Jed was always thinking about other people. Like the time he rescued Grum's prize cuckoo collection. Grump had given her most of the clocks when he was stationed in Germany after the war. Sentimental value didn't mean much to Pa. When he was moving Grum in with us, he threw her clocks in the dump heap even though Grum begged him not to.

"Don't be ridiculous, Mother," Pa argued, in what was, for him, a tender voice. "You know there's no room in the house for all your crap."

True, there wasn't any room. Between the windows, doors, and cupboards, we hardly had enough space for a calendar downstairs. Upstairs the house had mostly roof for walls, no place for clocks with pendulums that need to hang flat. The bunk beds barely fit in the window dormer.

"Where there's a will, there's a way, son," Grum said, with her chin trembling stubbornly. "You just don't want me to keep the clocks because you hate them."

Also true. We'd all heard Pa's funny stories about the

naughty things he'd done to silence the cuckoos when he was a kid. Like following Grum when she wound the clocks and unwinding them after her. Or jamming Popsicle sticks behind the birds when they popped out. Hanging the clocks upside down. No matter how many spankings he got from Grump, Pa kept trying to shut up the cuckoos.

Pa always got everybody laughing silly when he told his childhood cuckoo stories. The way he told them, it was hard not to laugh. He'd act out the parts, mimicking his little boy self and Grum and Grump like a comedian on TV. But if you really thought about what was happening, it wasn't that funny.

We waited nervously to hear what Pa would say back to Grum. He sucked on his teeth for a while before answering. "Mother, do you really think that if there was a way to keep those clocks for you, I wouldn't?"

Jed had been pacing around with his hands in his pockets, kicking rocks and acting like he wasn't paying attention, but he was really churning over every word. "Are you saying you would keep them, Pa, if we can find the space?"

"What do you think I'm saying!" Pa returned.

And that's when Jed came up with the idea of moving himself and Grum's cuckoos out to the castle. Pa benefited from the deal. He kept the couch.

Thinking about Jed and Pa and their disagreements made me wonder again which one was right about Stanley Odum. Now that an ORC sign had showed up on the commune door, I was starting to lean toward Jed. How could a bunch of people disappearing overnight be good? What kind of an offer couldn't they refuse from Boots Odum? What good could that guy be up to, mining mysterious rocks and keeping it all a big secret? On the other hand, Pa always said that there are some things we aren't supposed to know. For our own good. So I still wasn't sure who was right. But one way to find out was in my hand.

As I waited to fall asleep, I held Odum's blinky pebble next to my cheek. It felt warm and relaxing, like sucking my thumb used to feel before Pa trained me out of it. A memory popped into my head from when I was little, sitting on Pa's shoulders. It was just me and him working on the castle on a Saturday because Ma had taken Barbie to Daisy Scouts, and Jed was in the gore raking leaves for Grum.

"Whaddya say we put the finishing touches on this beauty and surprise the rest of the clan?" Pa had suggested, and now he was letting me place the last fieldstone in the vaulted ceiling. Best moment of my life so far.

It made my heart ache along with my stomach and teeth and growing bones to think about how Pa had changed. How everything had changed. Suddenly it was the present that didn't seem real . . . Grum tiptoeing around with her osteoporosis, Jed gone nobody knew where, Pa always blowing up, the house practically falling down around us, the gore nothing but churned dirt, to say nothing of eggs turning to stone and neighbors disappearing. And not a thing I could do to change any of it. So I didn't let myself think about the present. I just went back to putting the last stone in the castle.

Until I went flying.

Seriously! All of a sudden it was like I was sucked off Pa's shoulders and out into space. I couldn't see a thing. I couldn't hear, taste, smell—all I could do was feel myself flying in circles. First in one direction and then swinging the opposite way, like a figure eight. I couldn't see the shape, only feel it, because I was on the inside looking out, not seeing myself. The swooping went on and on until my whole body began to vibrate.

Finally, a familiar feeling. I knew exactly where I was. I was in bed, Ma shaking my shoulder in the gray light of a stormy morning.

"Sebby, Sebastian Daniels. Up'n at 'em!"

"Maaaaa-aaa! It's Saturday!"

"Chickens don't know that. And don't forget to close the doors."

Getting up was always a shock, but that day it was even worse, with the blankets pressing down on me, the light burning my eyes, the cigarette and mildew smells stinging my nose, and the cookie dough still bowling in my guts. For once I actually wanted to get up. Up and out of that suffocating house, away from Pa's jackhammer snoring. And forget that crazy dream. Man, it felt so real.

When I went downstairs, Ma was in her cloud of cigarette smoke, reading her Bible as usual early in the morning. But something was different. Her reading glasses. That was it. She didn't have them on, but she was staring at the page anyway.

I heard a little plop sound on the paper.

"Ma?" I looked at her. She didn't look at me. "Go do your chores, Seb." Her words sounded pinched.

"Ma, what happened?"

She didn't look up, didn't speak. There came another little plop, and this time I saw the tear glisten before sinking into the page she was reading.

Then I noticed something that made me feel like a big glass of ice water had been dumped over my head. The baggie with the egg in it sat next to Ma's Bible. Pa hadn't delivered it to the university after all.

"Oh, Ma, don't cry. It'll be all right." I didn't know that it would, but at the moment it was my job to make her feel better, not the other way around.

Pa had probably only made it as far as the Do-Drop-Inn last night. His truck had a hard time not turning in at the tavern. I knew, because I'd been with him more than once when an invisible power turned the steering wheel that way instead of toward the grocery store for milk. Ma must have been mad when he got home. They must have gotten into it. Maybe while I was stuck in that wild dream.

As I walked slowly to the door, the cold-water feeling was heating up fast inside me, boiling into anger. I wanted to run upstairs and pound Pa's face in while he slept. I wanted to grab a knife and stab him. I wanted him to hurt. No, I wanted him to never wake up. And then I wanted to puke because all those crappy feelings made me realize something.

The way I felt right then was exactly the way Pa talked a lot of the time.

I never get into fights with guys who pick on me at school, no matter how hard someone presses my buttons, because I'm afraid. Not afraid of getting hurt. Afraid of what I might do if I ever get started pounding on some bully. I get so mad, I might never stop. I just might pound and pound and pound until there's nothing left.

I could curl up and take a beating every day for the rest of my life, but that didn't change what I was inside. Inside, I was just like Pa. With that thought churning in my stomach, I went out to see how many eggs I could kick around today.

It was still raining hard, and I had to leap mud puddles on my way to the chicken coop. The water runoff had left mini canyons and craters all around the yard, so I had to watch where I landed.

When I opened the door, Barney greeted me with the wimpiest little *doodle-do* I had ever heard, and no hens took to the air. No hens sat on their nests. No hens were anywhere in the coop, and no eggs, either. Had a fox gotten in? But how? I hadn't left the outside door open yesterday. I hadn't! It was shut tight when I came in. I didn't see any signs of a predator. No clumps of feathers or trails of blood around, and we would have heard the commotion anyway. Once when a wild dog got a hen, Barney let the whole world know, and the hens joined in.

Those hens had to be around here somewhere. Probably had enough of me stealing their future chicks and snuck off to lay their eggs in a secret hidey-hole. Our hens never went far, though. They liked being fed. So out I went to look for them, in the pouring rain after all. Shoot. Why hadn't Ma told me to wear my raincoat? I grabbed an empty feed sack to hold over my head as I searched the chickens' favorite hiding places.

Nope, no sign of them under any of the bushes or the porch steps or perched on Jed's castle. Not even a lonely feather. And the dish next to the lawnmower was half full of Jed's Stupid Cat's food. The chickens would have cleaned that up if they'd gone near it.

Ouch. My stomach hurt. Those dough rocks were doing somersaults. Pa would blame me for this. He'd make me pay. Oh, I wished I knew where to find Jed. I'd run away and stay with him. He'd understand.

I was searching high and low for the third time when Barbie came outside—in her raincoat *and* carrying an umbrella. "Ma wants to know what's taking you so long. She wants the new eggs now so she can take them—hey, why are you looking at me like a beggar?"

"I'm dying of cookie dough poisoning. And all of the chickens have been kidnapped by Colonel Sanders."

"Sebby! You lost the hens? You're dead all right." She was looking under the porch. I was glad I had taken Odum's pebble to bed. Now it was safe in my pillowcase.

"I already looked *everywhere*. Three times. The chickens aren't *anywhere*."

"You look three times for your sneakers every morning, too, and they aren't anywhere in the house until someone else points at them." Yeah, that was true. My sneakers have invisible cloaking powers that only work on me.

She checked all the bushes and Jed's castle and the cat food corner, then she headed into the henhouse. I followed her. "Shish, there's no use. I'm telling you, they aren't—what are you doing?"

"What does it look like I'm doing?"

It looked like she was going to the feed closet at the back of the building, but there was no way the chickens could get in there.

"Why look there?" I said. "The chickens can't get in. I never, ever leave that door open, or the chickens would eat—"

I was interrupted by a howl and a blur of gray and white fur that shot out of the closet, between Barbie's feet, and out the henhouse door. Which I'd decided to leave open for the moment in case the chickens showed up and wanted back in.

"—everything. How did Jed's Stupid Cat get in there?"

"Gee, Seb, I don't know. Why don't you ask your sneakers?"

"But—"

"Sh!" Barbie put her finger over her lips and leaned into the closet. "Do you hear that?"

I listened hard, heard rain on the roof, heard myself breathing, and then I heard a pathetic faint *cluck . . . cluck . . . cluck*.

"Sounds like they're back behind all this mess of yours. Sheesh, Sebby, what do you do on Saturdays when you're supposed to be out here cleaning?"

"This is how I clean," I said with a shrug. Everything was

put away. So what if I didn't take the time to make it all neat like the Shish would. She even folded her socks. And put them in Roy G Biv rainbow order. My system wasn't fancy, but it was easy.

The closet was just barely longer than a bathtub, and wider, so you could walk in and reach the long shelves on the left side of the door. The closest shelves were for bales of clean hay, feed, and other chicken stuff. The far end held the plastic bins of Christmas decorations and other junk in storage. The open part near the door held the tall and wide things like the pitchfork, wheelbarrow, and a deep sink with a drippy spigot.

"Help me move this stuff," the Shish commanded. And I tried to help. I really did. But with each step I took toward the closet my stomach somersaulted harder. I felt like those dough rocks were going to pick me right up in the air and spin me in circles. "Ow, ow, ow, ow, ow!" I held on to the door and doubled over with the pain.

"Oh, *puh-leeze,* Seb. If you want me to help find your missing chickens so Ma won't kill you, you'd better cut out the melodrama right now. I'm serious." She crossed her arms to show me. But I wasn't acting, and the tears came to prove it. That melted her down.

"Sebby, what's wrong? Your stomach again?"

I nodded.

Barbie put her arm around my shoulders. I didn't push her away. I was really scared.

"We gotta go tell Ma. You probably need a doctor."

Probably. Except that Ma had enough to worry about. And I had other plans, too. Spying is hard to do in an emergency room. So I wiped my eyes. "No big deal. I'm fine. I'll just get some fresh air, and then I'll come back and help you."

The Shish looked doubtful, but she nodded. I took her

umbrella and went outside. The fresh air did help. My stomach went back to the same dull ache I'd been living with for a couple of days.

While I was out there, the Post Office truck came by, so I crossed the road to get the mail. Making myself useful. Ma and Grum would love that. On the top of the stack sat an envelope with the Mildew School logo in the return address. Uh-oh. The letter was addressed to Ma and Pa in the tiny, neat handwriting I saw on all my school papers. Ms. Byron. And then I remembered that she'd said she was writing home to my parents about my homework.

Suddenly a very unfortunate accident occurred. An ORC truck whizzed by with a whoosh of air that dragged the envelope right out of my hand. It tumbled like an autumn leaf into the ditch and sank into the frothy wastewater from the gore.

I'd have swum for it, honestly, but I couldn't keep Barbie waiting any longer.

◦ 8 ◦

By now Barbie had most of the closet emptied out in neat stacks. It seemed impossible that so much had fit into such a tight space, including the broken furniture and toys Pa was going to fix someday. Seeing the rusty red wagon he used to pull me and Barbie around in made me smile. Until I saw what was in it. Jed's protest signs. So much for smiling. Those signs depressed me.

Nobody in town liked what Boots Odum had done to the gore, but nobody hated it more than Jed. The week before he ran away, he had started a protest all by himself. He made picket signs and marched them back and forth across the main entrance to ORC. One read:

THIS NATURAL BEAUTIFICATION PROJECT
BROUGHT TO KOKADJO BY
OUR RICHEST CITIZEN

Another one had a picture of the gore from Kettle Ridge before ORC, all glorious with fall foliage and curls of wood smoke coming out of stone chimneys, most of which Pa had built. Then another picture of the same area stripped down to the crumbly dirt. The caption said:

DON'T YOU WANT TO KNOW WHY?

My favorite one was a picture of Boots Odum from one of his billboards, pasted next to a picture of Grum packing all her stuff up in garbage bags. It said:

WHAT DO YOU EXPECT
FROM A GUY CALLED "BOOTS"?
HE BOOTS PEOPLE.

That one was my favorite because it made you feel something, even if the sad little old raggedy lady wasn't your own grandmother kicked out of her home. But Grum was embarrassed when she rode by and saw Jed and his signs on her way to the church coffee klatch one day. "I wasn't booted, I was bought out," she said and made Pa stop the truck.

It wasn't pretty what Pa did to Jed right out on the street at the edge of town. Jed stayed to himself for a couple of days afterward, like always after Pa got after him. But then he up and disappeared.

It upset me terribly to see those signs again. I hadn't forgiven Pa yet for driving my brother off. I didn't know if I ever could.

"Hey, Seb, I can't see anything back here. Will you come back from Pluto and get me the flashlight?" Oh yeah, I was supposed to be helping the Shish look for the chickens.

"I'll get us a flashlight. Have to take the mail inside anyway."

"Well, hurry up. I still have my own chores, you know." She poked her head out of the closet. There were cobwebs all over her hair. It made me feel kind of affectionate toward her.

"Thanks, Barbie. Really," I said. I meant it, too. And then she had to go and say, "Don't tell Ma yet about having no eggs. We might find some when we find the chickens."

"Well, duh." Now Miss Smartypants was ticking me off. I

already knew that. After all, I was just as gifted and talented as she was.

"And don't tell her about the missing chickens yet, either." She pointed her perfect fingernail at me. Made me wish I'd broken it off when we wrestled yesterday. Anyway, instead of all the insults I was thinking, which would make her quit doing all the work, I just said, "Yes, your majesty."

The first thing Ma said when I kicked my way in was, "Seb, you have to stop giving milk to the cat. We can't afford it, and milk isn't good for cats anyway."

As usual on Saturday mornings, she was going through the cupboards and the coupons, making her weekly grocery shopping list. Pa was still jackhammering upstairs louder than the washing machine spinning in the basement.

"I didn't feed the cat anything," I said. "Must have been Barbie dumping her milk to get out of—"

Whoops, if Grum heard that, Barbie would be hearing from her, and then I'd be hearing from Barbie. I looked around and saw Grum on the couch grinning at the TV. It was quite a sight since she hadn't yet put her teeth in for the day. I had to find out what had made her gums so happy, so I headed for the couch to join her.

"Hold on, no TV for you yet," said Ma, grabbing me by the belt loop as I passed her. "Where are the eggs? And where's your sister? If she doesn't get her chores done pretty soon, there won't be any roller skating for you two this afternoon."

Oh, right. "She's actually helping me clean out the feed closet," I said. "We emptied it all out and we're going to reorganize everything. I came in to get a flashlight."

"Really!" Ma looked surprised and pleased. "Good idea! That closet does need a good reaming out. You can help Barbie clean the bathroom later, since she's helping you now."

“And I brought in the mail,” I said, pointing to the pile I’d left on the table.

“Why, thanks, Sebby,” Ma said with her sudden bright smile that always made me smile back, no matter how crummy I felt. Then her smile fell as she leafed through the envelopes. My heart stopped for a beat. Was she expecting the letter from school?

I cleared my throat. “Everything okay, Ma?”

She tried to bring back that bright smile, but this time it looked more like a wince. “Nothing for you to worry about, hon. It’s just the property tax bill. We’ll figure out how to get it paid, somehow. We always have.”

Our property went from the Zensylvania border down along one side of the gore, and then it crossed the road and wrapped around the narrow end of the triangle. The taxes on all that land were pretty high. Pa’d been after Ma to sell it and buy something cheaper near where she worked, and then she’d save money on gas, too, but Ma didn’t want to move. This place had been in her family for generations—the house tucked into a little niche in the ledge, plus a narrow stretch of mountain that rose almost straight up behind us. Ma loved this place, even if Pa was always calling it a worthless hunk of rock.

“Oh, Seb, is that the pebble Miss Beverly gave you?” Ma nodded toward a gray orb paperweighting the shopping list. “I found it in your pillowcase when I stripped the beds for laundry.”

“Looks like it,” I said with a gulp. Hoping my little pet had been behaving itself.

“I see why you like it,” she said. “It’s a soothing size and shape to hold.” She knew about my habit of falling asleep with a pebble in my hand. My heart beat fast as I waited for the “but . . . ,” but Ma just said, “Hurry up and bring me my eggs, sweetie.”

I put the rock in my pants pocket, and it started to vibrate a little. How annoying. As soon as I got outside I rolled it into my sock again so I could concentrate on the great chicken closet caper.

Barbie had finished clearing everything out. I went in with the flashlight on high, and the yellow arc lit up the problem loud and clear. A jagged black stripe had formed where the vertical barn boards were rotting away along the ground. The outline of the black mildew stain looked like half of a giant snowflake, symmetrical swirls branching down from each side of the center tall point.

"Look, there!" I said. In the middle of the jagged half snowflake I'd spotted a dark hole just big enough for a chicken to squeeze through. Or a cat!

Barbie lifted the shelves off their brackets to clear the way. "Give me the umbrella, Seb," she said with her hand out. She took it and started poking it through the hole. The metal tip clinked and clanked against something hard.

"Gee, I wonder what that is," I said, being sarcastic of course. The coop was built right up against the sheer face of a rock. Over the years, tree roots and undergrowth had filled it in at the sides and over the top to join the mountainside to the roof. It looked pretty, actually, almost like pictures of thatched cottages in storybooks.

Barbie kept clanking around, making the hole bigger. "If you really cared about those chickens, you wouldn't do that," I said. "You're going to Shish Kebarb them." Heh heh heh.

"Chickens should be smart enough to get out of the way," she said. "And besides, I'm just trying to find out if they're really back there. Why aren't they squawking and shuffling around?"

She was right. We both fell silent and listened. Rain. A car going by. The roof creaking. But not even a pathetic little *cluck*.

"Maybe they died," she said, putting her face down to the hole. "It smells musty and—something else. Can't put my finger on it. It's not a foul odor, though." Then she laughed. "God, I'm smart."

"Huh?"

"F-O-U-L, F-O-W-L?"

"Ha ha. If you were really smart, you'd try this." I handed her the flashlight. She blushed and said wittily, "I don't see how the chickens could even get back there anyway, with the closet door always shut."

I leaned closer as she aimed the light through the hole. A strange smell did come from there—sweet, almost. It reminded me of Ma's cookies baking. Ouch, that made my stomach ache harder.

"Oh my my my," Barbie said.

"Yup," I said.

At the edge of the flashlight's arc lay a pair of chicken feet, toes up in a pool of dark water.

I reached into the hidey-hole to pull on them. It hurt my stomach more the closer I got, but curiosity eased the pain. The chicken seemed kind of stuck. In fact, it seemed almost as if she was pulling on me! Mostly I felt it in my guts. That was one rugged bird. I braced my feet against the wall and pulled as hard as I could with both hands. The chicken made a hard banging sound as its body hit the wood. I gave it my best yank. Finally the whole board gave up and pulled away, sending me THWACK! against the wall. Barbie screamed.

"Don't worry, Shish, I'm all right. Not too sure about the chicken, though."

"I'm not worried about you. Look what's back there!" She

pointed at the opening. The broken board had pulled several other boards ajar, just like a door. Whoa, it *was* a door! And behind it, we found what we were looking for all right.

Chickens. Lots and lots of chickens, and a few eggs, piled every which way in the narrow space. Nothing moved, though.

"That," I said, "is really, really freaky."

"Are they still alive? Sebby, you check. I don't wanna touch them."

"I meant the door," I said, but I was still on my butt with a chicken between my sneakers, so I tapped on it with the broken board. The hen no longer had soft, giving feathers. They thumped.

That bird was petrified.

"Wow. And I thought the turkey Ma made for Thanksgiving was tough."

Barbie rolled her eyes at me. "So the chickens are all dead. We're gonna hafta tell Ma."

"Well of course."

We were both quiet a moment, staring at the rock chicken. I felt the absolute worst I had ever felt about being me, even worse than the moment I saw myself in the mirror at Odum's mansion. This was all my fault. I must have left the supply closet door open. I honestly thought I hadn't, but that's the only way the hens could have gotten in there. The chickens never got away when Jed was tending them. If only I could be more like him.

"You can tell Ma, Barbie," I said. "I'll be on my bike. On my way to Canada. You know Pa's gonna blame me for this, and I for one don't want to be around to see it."

"Me neither. Maybe I'll go with you."

We grimaced at each other. It was a moment of true desperation. I was briefly aware of kind of liking my sister, and sorry I got the curly blond hair she wanted, because straight and brown wouldn't have bothered me. The thought occurred to tell her about the Hole in the Wall. But I got over that quickly.

"Sebby!" Ma shouted from the kitchen door. "Don't make me come out there and get those eggs myself!"

"On the bright side, we found 'em!" I said to Barbie. "My stomach kills if I bend over in the closet. How about you throw me the eggs and I'll put them in the basket?"

She picked up the closest one and shook her head in wonder. "It looks perfectly normal, but it feels like a rock," she said, then pitched it to me like a baseball.

Man, I wished I'd had a glove on when it hit my hand. It smarted! And the egg didn't even crack! The instant I caught it, colors started shimmering in the shell just like Odum's pebble did when I held it. Come to think of it, that pebble was getting pretty worked up in my sock right now, pulling on my ankle like it was trying to drag me into the chicken pile.

I put the egg in the basket and stepped outside the closet. The egg and the rock both calmed down. Then I looked in at Barbie, hoping she hadn't seen any of the wondrous special effects. Luckily, she was leaning into the hole with the flashlight. Then she turned and pitched me another egg. My stomach lurched again, and suddenly I realized what was going on.

The cookie dough in my stomach was attracted to the petrified chickens and their eggs! And so was Odum's rock! They all had something in common. Something to do with the strip mine?

At that moment what I wanted more than anything was to figure out what Boots Odum was up to. And the last thing I needed was Barbie running into the house screaming about the magic evil that had possessed me. Ma would call the doctor and the minister and maybe even a lawyer, and then any chance of solving the mystery on my own would be all over. Odum would find out and make everything go his way.

To keep Barbie from seeing the eggs go Easter on me, I caught the rest of them in the basket as she threw them. It was the most fun I'd had all day. Then Barbie paused and said, "Aw!" in a sad kind of voice. "Come see this, Seb."

I leaned in as far as my cookie dough would let me and looked where she shone the light. On top of a hen sat a half-grown chick, not moving a feather.

"What if it's still alive?" she said.

"Pick it up and find out."

"No, you."

"Mister Sebastian Alfred and Miss Barbara Arleene, now!"

On the bright side, Ma was just screaming her lungs out from the front steps. The next stage would be, well, not worth going there. We had to hurry. "So, Shish, what do you want to do?"

With her toe she nudged at the chick until it lay next to the hen I'd pulled out through the door. Both of them stared at us like unwound cuckoos. "Aw," she said again.

"You know," I said, "it's not like telling Ma the whole truth now would bring her chickens back to life. We could wait until, say, after roller skating."

Skating is Barbie's favorite two hours of the week. It's the one thing that might tempt her to forget she's a goody-goody who would never expect Ma to waste her money on selfish fun when her only source of extra income was expiring behind the chicken coop.

"Hm. Yeah, it's bad enough that we have to hand her a basket of eggs that could be rocks. We should let her get used to that idea first. We can break it to her gently about the chickens."

"After Pa goes out," I added.

Miss Barbara Arleene Daniels smiled. I had her. “I’ll take the eggs in for you,” she said. “I still have to clean the bathroom, anyway.”

She didn’t need to know that Ma had told me to help her with that. “Good idea. I’ll stay out here and work on this mess.”

9

At Skate Away, you can lose yourself to the speed with the wind in your face. Your only problem is the people in front of you and how to aim yourself between them without knocking them over or slowing yourself down. It's great to be alive. But it's not so great to be in a crowd of people when you have a half-grown chick stuck to your belly. That's why, instead of buying tickets when we got to Skate Away, I steered Barbie out the back door. Where no one else could see my newest complication, I unzipped my raincoat and pulled up my hoodie to show her.

The chick she'd found in the hen pile faced her, sticking to my T-shirt like a magnet on a refrigerator.

"You freak!" Barbie yelped. She jumped back and rustled the shrubs. Water sprayed my face. And my chick. "No wonder you wore your raincoat to lunch. And Ma believed you when you said it was your *space suit*. Shouldn't you be in the hospital?"

"Don't worry, Shish. My cookie dough and my chick are very happy together." I patted the chicken's head dry. "It happened by accident when I was cleaning up the henhouse."

I was gonna toss the chick and that first chicken back where they came from, shut the door, and stack some junk on the shelves so there wouldn't be any explaining to do if Ma or Pa happened to come in. But the moment I picked up the chick, it felt like a magnet yanking on my hands. It flew itself to my stomach and stuck there. I pulled and pulled but it wouldn't budge. But I sorta didn't mind. It took my bad stomachache away. In fact, my stomach felt kind of happy, in a woozy driving-over-a-hill kind of way. But one small chicken on the stomach was enough. To play it safe I used a shovel to move the bigger one.

I wanted to explain all this to the Shish, except I had barely started the first sentence when she put her hands to her big open mouth and bit back a scream.

"Now what?" I said. I was losing patience.

"Did you see that? The chick's eyes moved! It's still alive!"

"You're nuts."

"Pet her head again and watch her eyes."

This time I bent my neck like Miss Beverly to get a view of the chick's face. "Awesome!"

"Only you would find this acceptable."

"Don't you think she needs a name now? How about Celery?"

"Why Celery?"

"After that science experiment when Ms. Byron had us put celery in colored water to show us how the Petrified Forest turned to rock. My celery turned blue the fastest. Remember?"

"And you can't remember that *is* is a verb! So, are you and Celery planning to live happily ever after, or are you going to let Ma take you to the emergency room like a sane person?"

"No, I want to go see Miss Beverly. She invited us back any time, didn't she?" While I talked I waved my hand back and forth in front of Celery, watching her eyes move. It was so cool.

"What's Miss Beverly gonna do? She's no doctor."

"But she'll let us into Boots Odum's house, and I have to find out what he's up to."

She just shook her head, staring at me and Celery like we were crazy.

"Well, hey, I'm the one with the chicken blinking up at me, not you. I'm going. You can come with me, or you can go skating. I don't care."

Without looking back at her, I headed off toward the bike trail that ran through the woods behind the businesses on Main Street. Pretty soon I heard feet squishing behind me on the wet ground.

"Does it hurt?" the Shish whispered. I was a tiny bit glad to hear her voice.

"No, it actually makes me feel better," I said, and explained everything as we trudged along. It didn't take long for my socks to get soaked up to my ankles because of the holes in my sneakers.

After a while Barbie said, "Look, there's Boots Odum's house." She pointed at some trees where the shingles showed between them.

As the path turned, the mansion appeared to grow in under the shingles. But the backyard didn't seem to belong to the front, it was such a mess. From the road you couldn't see the tumbledown stone wall, overgrown garden, old cars, boats, and other junk holding up weeds. At the end of a path to the house stood a weather-beaten barn that could have come from the gore, it looked so ramshackle. And suddenly, due to no plan of my own, I was heading straight toward it.

Celery and Cookie were pulling me by the stomach. I could either go where they wanted or hang onto a tree and scream. I had to pedal my legs hard to keep up with them.

"Seb, where do you think you're going?" Barbie yelled as I reached for the doorknob.

"In out of the rain," I said. I had a feeling that if I didn't open the door, I'd be stuck to it. Like Celery was to my belly. So I went inside and whoa!

A flash of rainbow colors flew across the room straight at

me. I turned around just in time for whatever it was to hit my back with a SPLAT! I doubled over screaming with the pain I expected to stab me. Only it didn't hurt at all. Celery stopped pulling so hard. My stomach felt swirly, however. Was I finally going to lose the dough?

Barbie slipped through the door. I turned around to show her what had hit me. She gasped. Again. She'd been doing a lot of gasping lately, and putting her hands over her mouth, like she was right now.

"How did that happen?" she said.

"What do you see?"

"It's that pattern again. The curlicues. Like the black marks on the henhouse wall. Except in color."

"Are you kidding me?"

"What did you expect? A picture of your chick from the back?"

I had to smile. That would make a good T-shirt. But Barbie wasn't smiling. "Let's get out of here, Seb!"

Instead I stepped deeper into the barn and looked around. What a mess! Books and papers crammed between piles of tools, gadgets, beakers, burners, and jars. Even in the bathroom. Walls plastered with maps and design drawings. Newspaper clippings. The cluttered desk had a bulletin board over it pinned with papers and pictures going every which way. A couple of the notes looked so much like Jed's handwriting that my heart skipped a beat. I took one down and studied it. It said:

HOW CAN YOU TELL IT'S RAINING CATS AND DOGS?
YOU STEP IN A POODLE

It even sounded like Jed! I guessed Boots Odum must have a decent sense of humor.

Littering the floor was a trail of empty Styrofoam cups cut from an egg carton, all stained like they'd had paint in them. Which they probably did before the colors decided to fly onto my raincoat. As I walked by them, they jiggled a little. One of them stuck to my sock like a burr. Yes, the same sock with my rock rolled up in it. I yanked the egg cup off me and tossed it into the garbage can. At least Barbie hadn't noticed—too busy peeking between the window blinds.

The trail of egg cups ended in front of the folding closet doors at the far side of the room, where a painting of a giant Easter egg sat on an easel. The egg was decorated with dozens of swirling curlicues made up of hundreds of swirling rainbows made up of thousands of millions and billions and trillions of colors, or at least it looked that way to me. The colors seemed to be in motion. "Is that what it looks like on my back?" I asked Barbie, pointing.

"Yyyeeesss. Can we go now?"

As I walked closer to study the details, a faint musical sound rang in my ears. Suddenly I felt like part of the painting, swirling among the colors, invisible. I vaguely sensed Barbie calling to me from far, far away. Then I felt a yank on my arm, but something stronger was pulling me toward the Easter egg. With a clattering sound, the canvas jiggled on the easel. Barbie gave up on pulling me and pushed the easel into the bathroom, then slammed the door and leaned against it.

"*Now* can we go?"

"Uh, yeah!" I wished. I stepped toward the entrance, but Celery wanted to follow the painting into the bathroom. She pulled, I pulled back, and we turned in circles like a corkscrew as Barbie nagged me to stop goofing off and hurry.

On one of my spins, the computer screensaver on Odum's desk caught my eye. My brother's cat! Or at least I thought so. Stupid's face flashed briefly on the screen, then split apart into dots and stripes that twisted and turned. Then they became the cat again.

"Quick, Barbie, look, it's Stupid!"

"What now? Everything's stupid to you."

"On the computer. It's Jed's cat! Oh yeah, that reminds me, Ma said to stop giving him milk. It'll make him sick."

"What are you talking about? I didn't give the cat anything."

"That's what I said. Must be Grum, then. She doesn't want Stupid to get osteoporosis."

"Well, I doubt that was Jed's cat you saw here, anyway," Barbie said.

By now the screen saver had moved on to other pictures. "Wait until it comes back around and you'll see," I said.

She crossed her arms and jiggled her foot nervously as she waited through photos of places around Kokadjo, B.O. and A.O. Meanwhile, I sat down—Celery didn't seem to mind that—and pawed through some things on Odum's desk, papers and books with big words I didn't get. I rifled through the closest science book.

"Shish, what's an isotope?"

"No clue. Look, Seb, waiting for the cat is taking too long. Can we go now?"

"What about turbulence? Or chirality?"

"That would be the sound your head will make when Boots Odum catches us in here. Will you hurry up?"

I spun the big globe on the desk. It had pins pricked into it here and there around the world. One was exactly where Kokadjo would be if Kokadjo were big enough to be on a globe. There were pins in every continent and ocean. Why had Boots Odum marked those places?

I jumped up to study the maps on the walls. One had a picture I'd seen in school of the continental divides showing all the tectonic plates. That map had a pin stuck in the Atlantic. And in very faint colored pencil lines, someone had drawn a swirling pattern with shading to make it look three-dimensional. Beginning at the pin and going underneath the ocean. All the way back to a pin marking Kokadjo. Around the edges of the map were newspaper clippings about natural disasters all over the world—earthquakes, volcanoes, tsunamis.

"Oh . . . my . . . Godzilla," I said. "Look at this, Barbie. Does this mean what I think it means? ORC's mining is causing all this damage!"

Barbie took a quick look and shook her head really fast. "No way," she said. "Impossible. Boots Odum is just . . . just an artist. A really good artist. This must be his plan for a painting."

The sketch was beautiful, just like all of the artwork Miss Beverly had shown us in the house. But what if it was more than that? What if whatever ORC was mining did have some powerful connection to other places in the world? It could be like when you pull a loose thread on the front of a sweater, and you wind up with a hole in the back. And somehow the cookie dough in my guts had put me in the middle.

Okay, now I was good and scared. "Hold the door, Barbie, I'm gonna make a run for it."

"About time!"

We'd have been out of there in a flash if a dog in the next yard hadn't picked that moment to start barking its head off. Was it barking at us, or was someone coming? I held my breath to listen.

Footsteps crunched on the gravel walkway leading to the barn.

༄ 10 ༄

"Hide! Someone's coming!" I said, looking frantically around the room. The closest escape was the bathroom with the painting that liked me. Not a good idea.

"In here!" Barbie slid open the folding closet doors at the far end of the workshop, and we burrowed into the hanging coats as the barn door creaked open.

"Stanley? Stanley?" Thank goodness, it was Miss Beverly. I pictured her twisting her sorry neck around, searching for him. "Good afternoon, dear," she said toward the bathroom door. Her voice sounded stretched out, worried. "Forgive me for intruding, but I heard you out here, and thought you could use a cup of coffee after being up all night trying to find an antidote for, you know. . . ."

She walked into the room, her footsteps creaking the wood planks, then lightly knocked at the bathroom door. I could hardly hear it with my heart thundering in my ears. I held my breath, hoping she wouldn't discover that Boots wasn't in the john after all. Even though his latest masterpiece was.

"I'm sorry, Stanley," she said with tears in her voice. "I know you told me not to use those eggs, but I thought you just meant for cooking. They were the only ones we had in the house, and they looked perfectly fine, so I didn't think it would hurt to use them in the balm recipe. Who would have thought it would . . . oh, please don't be mad. . . ."

Now I was holding my breath so I wouldn't miss a word.

Eggs? Our petrified eggs? Miss Beverly had used them, and now Boots was mad at her? Why? What had gone wrong? If I wasn't trespassing I'd have popped out and asked her.

Miss Beverly waited a moment, then sighed, and said, "Okay, Stanley, I'll leave you alone to work. Dinner's at six."

We would have been home free if Barbie hadn't picked that moment to let out her perfect bloodcurdling scream and bolted out of the closet. Straight into Miss Beverly.

Miss Beverly backed away, covering her face as if she didn't want to be seen, then uncovered, stood tall, and smiled meekly.

"Barbie!" she said. "Why, you gave me quite a scare! And Sebby! What are you kids doing here?"

I was fighting with the coat I'd been standing in, trying to get out of it, and tripping over all the junk in the closet. Milk crates and pails full of doodads, a bunch of furniture, and office supplies, just to name a few.

Miss Beverly seemed not just surprised, but nervous to see us. Her hand fluttered around the hair behind her right ear. Something about her seemed very different. She looked five inches taller, that's what! Most of it was her neck, sticking straight up.

"Miss Beverly! What happened to your . . ." Oops, I better not say hump. I didn't know what to say. Grum had told us enough times to go ahead and lie around the house slouching and not drinking our milk if we wanted our backs to look like question marks without answers for the rest of our lives. There wasn't any cure for osteoporosis.

From the top of her dahlia bulb nose to the bottom of her long, white, unwrinkled neck, Miss Beverly turned red. "It's, oh my, 'twas my own fault, really. Stanley warned me not to use the . . . , but, oh dear, I can't really say, I've said too much already. . . ."

She stepped outside, looked nervously around the yard, came back into the barn, shut the door behind her, and said, "You still haven't told me what you're doing here." With her long neck she looked ludicrous, like Alice in Wonderland when she grew tall.

"We actually came to visit you," I said, "and we—" I looked to Barbie for help, but she was looking warily into the closet. I was on my own. "We were on our way to see you and just stepped in here to get out of the rain."

Miss Beverly opened the blinds and let the sun in. "Would you like to try that again?"

Hey, when did the sun come out? The only thing I could think of to do next was cock my left eyebrow. A unique charm I got from Pa. He said the ol' Daniels eyebrow could get a fella anything he wanted from the ladies.

Sure enough, Miss Beverly melted into a smile. Then she looked closer at me and squinted. "Sebby, do you have something hidden under your raincoat?"

"What?" My hand went to Celery's head, and I imagined those chicken eyes moving. "Oh, that. It's . . . kind of embarrassing, actually. It's a . . . rare medical condition."

"Oh, dear. I'm sorry to hear that," Miss Beverly said. Then, after an awkward pause, "Look, you children are welcome to visit me at the house anytime, but Stanley doesn't allow guests in his workshop. He usually keeps it locked when he's not here. He must have gone off in a hurry. He did leave the place a sight." She stiffly bent to pick up the empty paint cups.

On her way to the garbage can she paused in front of the map with the swirling patterns sketched under the ocean back to Kokadjo. To turn her head she twisted her whole body around, not just her neck. "Such an imagination he has," she sighed, tracing her finger along the lines.

And then my sister surprised me. Instead of taking the chance to get out of there unscathed, she started pulling items out of Odum's closet, saying, "Sorry, Miss Beverly, don't worry, I'll put everything back. I just have to find out what bit me!"

Out came a lampshade, lawn chairs, computer parts, pails of rocks and bones—bones? no, fossils—while Miss Beverly fussed. "Something bit you? Oh, dear! But if you just . . . Barbie, please don't. Child, I wouldn't do that if I were you. Dear, if Stanley comes home and finds you—"

She put her hand to her heart and gasped.

"That bit you?" I said.

We were gaping at the statue of a poofy giant poodle. It would have been cute if not for the horrified look on its face, its mouth in a wide-open howl of terror. The dog was made of beautiful white stone, every hair carved in place, except for a missing tail and one broken ear, complete with severed blood vessels. The sculptor had a sick sense of humor. The details looked so real, my skin prickled with the heebie-jeebies.

Barbie was blushing now. "Well, my hand definitely got caught in some teeth. Sorry, Miss Beverly." And she hustled to bury the dog again.

Miss Beverly started to shake her head but stopped and put her hand to her neck, her lips set in a grim line while I helped Barbie return everything the way we found it. All but one thing that might possibly have fallen into my raincoat pocket. And then Miss Beverly shooed us out. I stayed as far away from the bathroom as possible, just in case Celery still had any funny ideas about getting together with the Easter egg.

On my way past the computer, the screen saver flashed a photograph that made me jump. It was Miss Beverly when she was younger, at a dog show with a blue ribbon around her neck and a poofy giant poodle licking her face! A dog that looked just like the statue! Yikes! Get me out of here!

I was a superhero blur of motion. Celery didn't have a chance to resist.

Miss Beverly walked with Barbie to meet me at the front gate. "You'll have to come back soon for some Easter candy," she said, feeling her neck and massaging the back of it with her fingers. Her eyes had welled up with tears. I felt bad for her.

"Does your neck hurt?" I said.

She made a painful noise that I took as a yes.

"I know how you feel," I said, my arms over my chick bump. "I've had a stomachache for days from eating raw cookie dough."

Miss Beverly blinked hard, took a tissue from her housecoat pocket, and dabbed her eyes. "Raw cookie dough? Sebby, that's not good for you!"

"Oh, he knows," Barbie said.

Miss Beverly used the tissue to blow her nose, sniffed, and said, "Stanley will figure out how to set things right. He always does."

The wind shifted, shaking the leaves overhead and sending a burst of water down on us.

"See? It was raining." I gave her the charming Daniels eyebrow again. She smiled a little. Pa was still good for something.

By now it was almost time for Ma to pick us up. As we ran back to Skate Away, Barbie said, "This one time I won't tell on you, Seb, because I'd get in just as much trouble for going along. But don't expect me to cover for you. You'd better get a story ready for when Ma asks what happened to your raincoat. Or why you suddenly have a twin chicken. Or what's in your pocket."

Innocently I peered down around the chick bump to the lump in my telltale pocket. Oh, booger. I didn't want Barbie to notice that. She has a little problem whenever I borrow stuff without permission. Even if it isn't her stuff.

"Don't worry, Shish," I said. "If Boots still needed these, he wouldn't have left them with a bunch of fossils in his closet, would he?" I pulled out the broken glasses and showed them to her. They only had one arm. Except for the cracks in the thick, milky lenses, they looked like the ones he'd put on to gaze around our yard the day he stopped for eggs.

She pushed my hand away and peered over her shoulder, as guilty as if police were watching us from behind every tree. "Oh, Sebby. Wasn't it enough for you to walk away with his paints?"

"Very funny," I said, scrunching my shoulder blades. My back tingled where the paint had landed. It felt kind of nice, like a massage.

Getting into the SUV I made sure Ma didn't see my back with the new improved color scheme.

"Did you have a good time skating?" she asked.

Barbie stared at me with her arms across her chest. She'd never tell a lie.

I avoid lying whenever and however possible. "Oh, Ma, you know we always have a good time when we go skating."

"Awww, that makes me happy," said Ma. "Money well spent. And speaking of spending money, while I was at the grocery store I noticed a big empty space on the shelf where the Zenwater usually is."

"See?" I gave Barbie a so-there punch in the arm. "Not only did the Dogstars disappear, so did their business. Now aren't you worried, Shish?"

"I wouldn't worry yet," Ma said. "The cashier said they were just sold out. The water is on backorder. She hadn't heard any rumors about the Dogstars."

Barbie punched me back and said, "And anyway, if the

Zenwater really is contaminated, doesn't that explain why they left so fast? I sure wouldn't want to live there anymore. Take the money and run."

"Good point, Barbie," Ma said. "I hope the Dogstars took Boots to the cleaners."

Good point, Barbie, nyah nyah nyah. After that I gave quite a bit of thought to her advice about getting a story ready. For about sixty seconds. Before I fell asleep. I awoke when the car came to a jolting stop and Ma said, "What the heck is *he* doing here?"

∽ 11 ∾

It was none other than Boots Odum, sitting in his shiny truck with a phone to his ear. When we got out of the SUV with our plastic grocery bags, he hurried over to help Ma. He carried six bags on two fingers of his right hand—the same fingers he had fluttered at me the day he came for eggs. What was it with those fingers?!

Pa yanked the door open for us. He had on his dress pants, a clean collared shirt, and a bodacious grin. The house smelled like apple pie, and it wasn't even Thanksgiving. Something was going on.

"Well, if it ain't Mr. Stanley Odum," Pa said. As if it was a big surprise to him. "Come on in and have a seat."

The room filled with Boots Odum's heel clacks. The smell of leather joined the crowd of bleach and mustiness and apple pie. Pa had already dragged the comfortable living room chair over to the head of the table. Barbie started putting away groceries. I ran upstairs and pulled on two loose sweatshirts to hide Celery, then slipped onto the bench at the far side of the kitchen table behind the empty egg basket. Normally Barbie would have manipulated the situation so I'd have to help her put the groceries away, but she took pity on my secret predicament.

"Thanks for calling last night to warn me about the eggs, Claire," Boots Odum said, pulling two empty egg cartons from his rucksack and holding them out like a sacred offering. "Don't worry yourself about a refund. We'll find a use for the eggs. They'll make good anchors for a space ship." He smiled proudly at his joke.

Pa guffawed and rubbed his hands together. "Claire, pour this gentleman a cup of coffee and cut him a piece of that delicious apple pie my mother made. Fresh out of the oven."

Ah, so. Grum was in on it, too. Whatever *it* was. But she was nowhere to be seen.

Boots Odum rubbed his hands together eagerly and said, "Don't mind if I do!" After an awkward pause, he added, "Enough rain for you folks?"

"Have a look in the basement, Stanley, and see for yourself," said Ma. There was no missing the edge in her voice, blaming him. She slammed a huge steaming mug in front of Boots Odum. Coffee spilled.

He looked around helplessly. Barbie tossed him the roll of paper towels off the counter.

"Thanks, cutie. Now, Claire, isn't the sump pump I sent over doing the job for you?"

Ma took a deep breath and said, "How much sludge could a sump pump pump if a sump pump could pump—"

Pa cleared his throat and laughed. His voice sounded higher than normal. "All Claire means is, we do get a lot of water when it rains. An old house. You know."

Odum nodded. "No offense, Craig, but I think Claire means it's my fault that water runs off the gore into your basement." He reached out to stop the dish of pie Ma slid down the table at him. "No eggs in this, I hope?" he said, winking at her.

She winced a sickly smile. I held my stomach. Well, technically I held Celery. Then I picked my pie apart and studied the apples for penicillin. Grum wasn't big on cutting out the spoiled parts.

Boots Odum took a long time chewing and rolling his eyes around ecstatically before he swallowed his first bite. "Yummee! Your mother-in-law's quite the cook, Claire. She always was. I'll never forget the brownie bribes she used to give Craig and me to stay out of her hair when we were little ruffians." He showed us all a smile with a big scoop of friendly on top of the rich and powerful. Ma fake smiled back.

"Too bad the ol' lady's not here to hear you say that herself," Pa said. "But I just delivered her over to the church for the weekly gossip." He grinned.

"Nobody's busier than a retired widow." Boots Odum winked.

"Cut to the chase, Stanley," Ma said, lighting a cigarette. "You didn't drop by to make small talk. Why *are* you here?"

"A woman who doesn't waste time. You're a lucky man, Craig," Boots Odum said and, grinning Pa straight in the eye, reached into his rucksack to pull out a loose pile of green and white. Cash.

Me and Barbie gaped at each other across the kitchen as she put a fresh gallon of milk away. Then I stared back at Boots Odum's hands because I'd noticed something strange as he neatened the stack of hundred dollar bills. His left hand looked a lot like Pa's, hairy and sinewy with veins popping out. But his right hand was as smooth as a mannequin's!

He caught me staring and gave me his little two-finger hummingbird wave. "It's bionic," he said, then placed the stack on the table between Pa and Ma.

"The money's all yours, Craig. And Claire. Right now, if you want it. All you have to do is sign your deed over to ORC. I'd like to see you in a more comfortable place as soon as possible. And to help you move, you can have use of an ORC company van and a couple of men with strong backs, gratis. No charge."

"Is that what you said to the Dogstars?" Ma asked. "I went up there last night to warn them about the eggs and saw your sign on the door."

"You did?" said Pa.

Odum nodded. "I'm aware of that, Claire, and I'm prepared to let the trespassing go, since you didn't realize the property had changed hands. No hard feelings. We're all friends in this town. So, what do you folks say? My people will help you move any time you're ready."

Pa stared down at the Ben Franklins, licking his lips. No apple on them, either. Ma glared at him, her lips tight over her teeth. I could see the fight behind her eyes. But would she say what she was thinking? Would she dare? In front of us, in front of Boots Odum? Ma's careful with what she says. You can almost see her weighing her words in her hands, the way her fingers knead at each other while she thinks.

Ma leaned forward. She took a deep pull on her cigarette, blew a sharp stream of smoke out the side of her mouth, and said, "Tell me something, Stanley. Can you sleep at night?"

"Like a log," he said. "I'd say like a baby except they wake up every two hours."

Pa cracked up at that. He says it himself all the time.

Odum put his hands behind his head, leaned back a bit, and said, "That's a strange question, Claire. Why would insomnia want to take hold of me?"

"Oh, I thought maybe you might have a pang of conscience over turning a beautiful chunk of nature into a cesspool, ruining the lives of your friends and neighbors, a few little things like that."

"Well, now." Boots Odum cleared his throat and looked at Pa as if to say, "Will you shut her up?" Pa was just staring at the money, hardly even listening.

Our visitor went on, "Claire, you *are* my friend and neighbor, and that's exactly why I'm here, offering you more money than you could ever get from this place on the conventional real estate market. Kokadjo is one heckuva fine community and I want to keep it that way by helping you folks out."

Ma shook her head, laughing. "Help us *out* is right, Stan. Do you really think anyone's buying your baloney? You're throwing money around hoping you won't get sued!"

Way to go Ma, I thought. Jed would be so proud! I was grinning inside, until I caught the look on Pa's face. It was red, ripe, and ready to pop.

"Claire!"

"Craig?"—and then she said with her eyes, *Don't you dare raise your voice to me in front of a visitor.* When he blew his stack at her, she always made him take the argument behind closed doors or else made us kids go outside.

I'd rather be out at the Hole in the Wall, anyway. I started to stand up, but Ma stuck out her arm and held me down in my seat.

"There's nothing wrong with raising your voice when you're good and mad!" Pa yelled. "This man is laying cash money on the table, and you're treating him like a criminal!" Then he took a quick look at the man. Boots Odum was frowning—just a little—but definitely frowning.

When Pa continued he wasn't loud, but with his face so stiff and his words so pointed, you knew it had to be paining him to keep the anger down. "Listen here, Claire. Be reasonable. We can trust Stan. Him and I go way back. You know that."

Ma tipped her head toward the stripped gore. "Back there?" she scoffed. "Nothing there to go way back to. It's as bad to rape the land as it is to do it to a person. And you know what else? The son-of-a-gun killed our chickens!"

Barbie dropped a roll of toilet paper as she was putting away bathroom stuff. We *uh-oh* looked at each other.

I swallowed hard. "Gee, Ma, what makes you think that?"

"Well, if he didn't kill the chickens, he might as well have. After I dropped you kids off skating I came back here to get one. Thought I'd take it to the vet. Couldn't find a single chicken—which I'm sure you two know very well and were afraid to tell me this morning." Ma pointed the finger of shame at us. "Dead or alive, it's pretty obvious what happened. *Someone* who doesn't want us to know what's wrong with them absconded with those hens!" She gave Boots Odum a full-on glare.

Boots Odum was literally taken aback—his chair almost fell over. The guy was shocked at the accusation, and I knew why, but I didn't dare tell Ma what had become of her birds. Not in front of Odum. Or Pa. I was still figuring on breaking the news to her gently. Eventually. After I followed through on an idea I had involving the glasses I'd borrowed.

Barbie opened her mouth but no words came out.

Boots Odum rebalanced himself and took a couple of deep breaths before he spoke. "Claire, those are very strong words." He used one of his bionic fingers to scratch his head in confusion. "I honestly have no idea whatsoever where your poultry have flown off to. And I assure you that I do not break laws; therefore, it would be useless for anyone to sue me. But I hear you, and I want you to know that ORC will be restoring the gore to a pristine public park when our mining interests are through. I mean it. Trust me, it'll be nicer than it ever was. There'll even be a lake."

"Hear that?" snapped Pa. "There'll even be a lake! You always wanted to live on the water, sweetheart."

"We already do," I muttered, rolling my eyes toward the cellar.

"A fat lot of good that lake'll do us if we sell out, Craig," Ma snapped back at him. Then she turned to Boots Odum. "Look, Stan, I believe you have grand plans and good intentions the way you see it. But the way I see it, there's no way you can succeed. Once you tear the world apart, you can't put it right. What you patch back together will be a different world entirely, with ugly spots and weak seams." She glanced at Pa then, with a look that made me wonder which one of them she was really talking to.

"Claire, you're not making any sense," Pa said. "Stan's talking straight business, not namby-pamby. You're just being stupid. We won't need your diddly buck fifty for eggs if we take Stan's offer."

"Stupid," Ma echoed in a hurt version of his sneering voice. "Diddly."

"Stupididdly," Pa repeated, his face arrogant. Ma looked crushed. I was stunned at the line he had crossed, insulting Ma like she was the same to him as Jed's Stupid Cat. And in front of us. How could he?

Ma looked out the window and blinked a few times, then said softly, "Stan, I know this place is just a hole in the wall. Some would say it ain't worth nothing. But to me it's everything. My kids were born here. I was raised here like generations before me. You want us to leave our family memories behind, for what? For money?"

Boots Odum leaned toward Ma, his face all sympathetic, and touched her arm gently. "You're right to love your home, Claire. But there's nothing wrong with change, either."

Ma got up from the table and turned her back as he went on.

"The land changes all the time, everywhere, in floods and fires and big winds, sometimes for the worse, sometimes for the better. And yes, sometimes you have to tear down the old to build a better new. Why, I can do more with my new hand than I could with the one I lost!"

I wondered how he'd lost his hand, but I didn't let myself ask.

Pa nodded. "Didn't Frank Edwards build himself a mini-mart with the money he got for his little shack in the gore?"

"Indeed," replied Boots Odum. "Also, the Pauleys opened a McDonald's, Elsa Beck opened a Montessori school, and some of the others are pitching in to build a mall. They'll start construction this summer."

"Did you say *mall?*" Barbie blurted. She'd finally finished putting the groceries away and was shoving me aside to get a seat on the bench.

"On the road to Exton. In fact, I can recommend a lovely new development near there that has homes for sale in your price range. Four bedrooms, two and a half baths . . ." He lifted the rucksack. "Take this money, Claire, and buy yourself a better life on the other side of town. Heck, set up a shop in the mall." His voice was sincere. Patient. Enticing.

The rucksack emptied out onto the table. Wads of Bens spilled in all directions, a mass of green faces.

"You've sold me," said Pa.

Ma turned an angry look on him, shook her head, and ground out her cigarette.

Odum kept talking. "What's your dream, Claire? Can you look me in the eye and tell me you don't have a dream that can come true when I wave this magic wand?" He picked up a stiff hundred, waved the bill around, and handed it to Pa.

Pa sniffed it. "Abracadabra and presto!"

"Here's what I think of your dirty money, Mr. Stanley O-dum Mud-o," I whispered in Barbie's ear as I folded one of the bills into a paper airplane. Then I looked at Pa, scared he would flip, but he hadn't seen me. Too busy staring at the bill in his own hands.

Ma ignored the money, glowering at Odum as she paced along the kitchen counter, trailing her hand along the edge.

"If you don't want to live in that development near the mall, Claire honey, we could move to that lake on the other side of Exton, closer to your work," Pa said sweetly. "Remember how much fun we used to have taking the kids camping at the state park over there?" He gave Ma the ol' Daniels eyebrow. Then I felt like a real jerk for using it on Miss Beverly.

For once the brow failed. Ma worked her jaw like a baseball player getting ready to spit a wad of chew.

"We can't afford to move to that yuppie neighborhood. It'd take a fortune just to pay the property and income taxes. This is a pile of cash, but it's no dream come true."

Boots Odum shifted his chair to the side, opening the circle to Ma. "There's more where this came from."

"Really!" said Pa.

"You think everyone has a price, don't you?" Ma said disgustedly. Her hands trembled as she knocked her pack of cigarettes on the counter and took one out. Boots Odum offered a lighter but she waved it away and lit her cigarette on the flame of the gas stove. "Stan, how about you just pay to send your nasty mine water somewhere else? Then replace my laying hens, repair the water damage to our home, and leave us alone."

"Yeah!" I blurted without thinking.

Pa looked up at me in surprise, as if I was a boil on his bottom he'd forgotten existed until he sat down. "You kids get outta here right now! This ain't none of your business."

Barbie was already on her feet. I started to go with her, but then I saw the phone on the wall and remembered Jed. If we moved, he'd have no place to come home to. We'd have no castle to remember building with Pa. No way to get to the Hole in the Wall ever again. Ma was right. No amount of money was worth losing those kinds of things.

"No," I said again, even though I knew what I'd be in for later. Pa didn't abide back talk.

"No? No what!" His face twisted something ugly.

"No, it's my life too, and I don't want to leave." I sat back down. Barbie, looking terrified, hovered at the stairway. But she didn't leave the room.

Me and Pa glared at each other, breathing hard, until Ma put her hand gently on his shoulder. "Your son has a point, Craig."

Pa shrugged her hand off. Suddenly the house fell so quiet, the refrigerator sounded like a bulldozer.

Boots Odum cleared his throat. "Well, I guess I'll leave you folks to talk it over."

He calmly collected his cash and went to the door. Which Barbie lunged ahead of him to yank on. It took her a few tries, with Boots looking embarrassed. He reached his bionic hand out and back and out and back, as if he wanted to do the job himself, until the door finally jolted open with a wooden scream.

Outside on the steps he turned to face us, the wind whipping his hair to the far side of his bald spot, his nose blooming red. "Claire, you know the value of what I'm offering. It's for your own good, trust me!" He sounded almost desperate when he said that. As if there really was more to it than business.

Then his face reset to powerful mode and he said, "Craig, when you can get your wife to talk sense, we'll talk dollars."

"Get off my property!" cried Ma, shutting the door in his face.

As soon as the truck motor revved outside, Pa pushed his chair back and got up, his hands on his belt, fingering the buckle as he glared at me. I knew what was coming. I made myself small in the corner and covered my head with my arms.

"All right, Mr. No. You had to go and make me discipline you. When are you ever gonna learn to respect your elders?"

Through my fingers I watched the leather slide through the first loop as he pulled on the buckle.

"Oh, stop that, you big bully," said Ma, grabbing the tail end of the belt. "I've had enough of you taking your frustrations out on these kids."

Barbie was about to shoot up the stairs, but Ma caught her by the arm and pulled her close, facing out. Barbie's face was all pinched and twitching like a cornered rabbit that sees the fox creeping up on her.

Then Ma pulled Pa around by the belt so he was facing her. He seemed even more surprised than angry. Ma had never defied him around us kids. They always stuck together, which usually meant Ma getting behind Pa. Well, now she was in front of him.

"Look, Craig. Look at your perfect daughter."

"Claire, you better—"

"Listen to me. I got something to tell you. See the fear in her eyes, Craig? She's so scared of you she'll be having nightmares tonight, only you won't know because you'll be passed out drunk while she's screaming and crying."

Pa scrunched his face at Barbie, then turned back to Ma. "You got no business dragging the kids into this, Claire. You're the one who's always saying—"

"I'm not finished, Craig. Just listen." Suddenly she had me out of my corner, locked against her chest, her heart throbbing in the back of my neck.

In the mirror on the opposite wall she looked like one fierce mother hen with her wings sticking out. I crossed my arms over the real chick. It didn't really show under the two hoodies

I had on. During all the Odum excitement I'd forgotten about Celery. She felt right at home on my stomach, and it enjoyed having her.

"Look at Sebby, your beloved son. Oh, he made you the happiest man on earth the day he said his first word, and it was *Pa-pa-pa*. He adores you back, or he would, if he wasn't trying so hard to hate you so you can't hurt him anymore."

Pa glared at me, then doubled his glare back on Ma. "Are you trying to tell me I don't love my kids? You're cracking under the strain, Claire. You need help."

"Funny, I was just gonna say the same thing about you." Ma's chin dug into the top of my head. I felt the vibrations of her voice in my skull as she talked, and it felt good. It helped me not to cry. Barbie was crying, softly.

Pa took the Lord's name in vain and said, "Are you done yet?" The phone rang. Nobody moved to answer it.

"No! You got one more person to look at, Craig, and it can't be Jed since you already chased him away. It's you. What happened to the man I married? The gentle and funny and responsible man? I want him back, or I want you out." Her voice wobbled around but she held the words together.

Pa was pacing, pacing as she spoke. For the first time in my life I wondered if he would hit Ma. I puffed my chest out to get in his way.

"Now you done?" His words were clipped. The phone rang on, a shrill scream.

"Yep. Your turn, Craig. I'm listening."

But Pa didn't say another word. He yanked the door open and slammed it behind him. Ma let us loose. Barbie ran upstairs. I got the phone.

It was Grum, wondering if anyone planned to pick her up or if she should get in line at the homeless shelter.

꩜ 12 ꩜

As soon as Ma left to get Grum, I pulled out Odum's glasses and put them on, mimicking his big smile. I was glad to have something to take my mind off the big scene that had just unfolded.

The house didn't look any different through the glasses. Except it had even more cracks in the walls. Wait, those were the cracks in the lenses.

I stepped outside. The yard looked the same as it had an hour ago. I scanned the gore. No difference. Then I turned in a circle and looked all around, up and down the mountainside our yard is tucked into. Same. Same. Whoa, different! In a puddle of water next to Jed's castle, I saw a faint blink. And another. And another. It made a swirly pattern of colors, maybe a yard long and an inch wide. Like a graffiti doodle swimming along. Unbelievable!

I took the glasses off and looked again. Just a normal mud puddle. Glasses on, blink blink blink. Like a winding trail of Christmas lights ending at the henhouse.

The henhouse!

In no time I was inside there, emptying the shelves in the supply closet so I could scan the mildewed wall.

"Ohmygodohmygodohmygod!" I couldn't stop saying it even though Grum's voice in my head was telling me I was probably causing a car crash somewhere by distracting the Lord's attention. Through the glasses I saw specks of color moving around in the jagged black half-snowflake shape.

"What? What is it, Seb!" The Shish had followed me.

"I'll show you in a minute," I said and pulled open the hidden door.

Immediately I saw one blink after another, all different colors in the rock cliff. Or was it in the chickens? I didn't get a chance to figure it out because I felt an irresistible pull on my stomach—Celery? Yes, she must be trying to get back to her flock, somehow. Before I could get a grip on the doorway to hold myself back, she had pulled me right up against the wall with all the other chickens.

Now I could see that they weren't just piled up—they were *stuck* there. Like magnets. I could also see that this wall wasn't just one slab of mountainside. It was a stack of fieldstones like we'd dug out of the yard to make the castle—a retaining wall without mortar. Somebody must have built it. Maybe Pa, back in his masonry days? But why do that in a place that nobody would ever see?

"Sebby, get out of there!" Barbie cried. "You're scaring me."

I was scaring me, too. Kicking and screaming, I pushed against the rocks with all my strength. And down fell the wall, Sebby and all.

Luckily none of the rocks landed on my head. A chicken foot scraped my elbow, though. The air suddenly smelled strongly like Ma's tooth-breaking cookies. Then I noticed a cold tug on my face. A breeze. This must be the entrance to a tunnel!

Barbie overcame her terror and leaned in to ask if I was all right.

"No! I lost the glasses!" I cried, groping around for them.

"Wait, I'll find the flashlight so we can see what we're doing."

But I kept groping around and found the glasses first.

Man-oh-man, I could hardly believe what I saw! I was looking down a long wall of blinking curlicues. It was like one never-ending paisley tie. And of course I had to find out where it led. It's not as if I had a choice. Celery had the same idea. And so did Jed's Stupid Cat. To my surprise, he came leaping in over the rocks, weaved a figure eight around my legs, and took off ahead of me down the tunnel.

The Shish chased after us with the dim flashlight bobbing. "Sebby, slow down. What are you seeing with those glasses? I want a turn!"

I would have been happy to slow down if I could. It was like the bird on my belly was flying me, even though she had rocks for wings, and the rock in my sock was helping. I'd forgotten it was there before, but now all of a sudden it was making me feel like that mythology dude with wings on his ankles. The feeling reminded me of that dream I'd had, being sucked off Pa's shoulders onto an invisible carnival ride. My sister wouldn't react well to hearing that I was being propelled by a force beyond my control, so I just ignored her.

"Argh! You are such a pain, Sebastian Alfred Daniels!" Her feet pounded faster and the next thing I knew, she'd ripped my ear off. Well, that's what it felt like when she grabbed the glasses.

Without them, the walls fell into dark shadow, all normal in the bouncing halo of the flashlight. Barbie looked comical with those pearly glasses perched at a cockamamy angle with no dahlia bulb to hold them up. Her nose is more like a clothespin. She used her free hand to prop up the side with no arm, and then she started oh-my-godding at the colors, too.

The tunnel twisted like a giant wormhole through the same kind of stone as the Hole in the Wall. Water streamed along the lowest curves in the floor. In some places it collected in pools that we had to pick our way around or jump over. Jed's Stupid Cat was great at avoiding the water. I just followed him.

"Where do you think this tunnel ends?" Barbie asked.

"Only one way to find out." And my two flying escorts weren't about to let me turn back, anyway. But I didn't tell my sister that.

The tunnel stretched really tall in some places and almost narrowed shut in other places. We had to climb over a few boulders. Occasionally another tunnel would branch off, but there was only one vein of curlicue colors, and we all wanted to go that way. Especially Celery.

Every time it was my turn to have the glasses, the deposits of color seemed thicker and brighter. The air smelled more and more of that sweet aroma, too. But it was so quiet inside the tunnel, it seemed the world outside had vanished. All we could hear besides ourselves was water dripping. Until a rumbling noise came out of nowhere, and just as suddenly was gone. And then it came and went again.

Dynamite! Odum's goons were mining here! Suddenly the tunnel crackled overhead. Dust fell in my eyes. Some small rocks thunked down around us. In my final thoughts I begged God to hurry up and forgive me for lying to Ma and let me get into heaven.

"Did you hear that, Seb?" Barbie said. "Sounds like cars whooshing by. I think we're crossing under the road."

Phew, reality.

In my head I drew a map of where we'd started and where we'd twisted and turned. "If there's a road going over us, we must have gone past the gore."

"Right," said Barbie. "Otherwise there'd be no tunnel. ORC mined all the rocks."

And then suddenly the tunnel branched again. This time

the colors went both ways, according to Barbie (she had on the glasses). "Which way should we go?" She stopped at the Y to ponder, but Celery and the pebble didn't need to think about it. They lurched to the right and sped me up as if we were going downhill, even though we were slanting upward.

At that I knew exactly where we must be. "We just rounded the pointy end of the gore!" I called over my shoulder. Barbie was pretty far back.

And then my sock gave up its heroic effort. The pebble burst out and did that spin-around ringing thing on the floor, like on the asphalt up at Kettle Ridge. Except this time it didn't stop and sit still. It kept spinning in loops down the tunnel like it wanted to chase Jed's Stupid Cat, and it was making that wind-chime noise! I tried to follow, but I felt like I'd just gotten off a carnival ride and was tripping over my own feet. The pebble wobbled around a curve and I lost sight of it in the darkness.

We had reached a huge cavern, from what I could tell by the tired flashlight. The light didn't reach any walls. I couldn't hear my pebble anymore, either, so gave it up for lost as Barbie came around the corner oohing and ahhing in the dark like it was the grand finale on the Fourth of July. "You have to see this! Seb, these glasses are magical. This *place* is magical!"

Maybe she was right. Because something in that cavern was giving me a funny feeling. My ears rang. My nose filled with that strong perfume smell. I trembled all over. I felt so hot and sweaty that I tore off my two hoodies. My hands shook as I held the glasses to my face, nervous about what I'd see when I got them on.

I didn't make a sound, though, because no air could pass by the lump in my throat. Beautiful! It wasn't just curlicue strings of light anymore. All the rock here seemed to be alive, swirling deep down with patterns just like the ones in Odum's paintings. The whole cavern was drenched with moving colors. They were bright and they were everywhere, even the floor and the ceiling. It made me think of a fairy tale dragon's lair filled with jewels.

For the first time since we'd entered the tunnel, Celery seemed happy to stay still. Everything felt right in the world. Solid. Permanent. I could have stayed in that moment forever.

"We like it here, don't we, Celery?" I petted her head. "Whoa!"

This was the first time I'd looked at her through the glasses. She was one fancy bird! Her plumage looked alive with colors. Then my stomach started to tickle, as if Celery was moving her feathers. Wait—she was! She was actually moving! And all of a sudden, so was my stomach, on the inside.

"Ow!" I bent over doubled with the pain. Celery fell to the ground, but she didn't hit like a rock. Her feathers fluttered and—holy bat cave! I couldn't believe it!—colors swirled up out of them and curlicued their way into the floor.

"Do you see that, Barbie?"

"See what? Your chick having a fit?"

I handed over the glasses and let Barbie watch while I held my stomach. Meanwhile, Celery's feathers twitched and plumped. Her feet did a little dance. She squawked and tried to fly.

I was filled with a wondrous dizzy feeling from head to toe. Especially in my stomach. And my back. Which was starting to itch like crazy. I pulled off my last shirt, the one I'd been wearing when Celery got attached to me. Barbie started talking a mile a minute about the colors coming out of *me*, but I didn't hear much because my head was filled with another noise of my own making. There's no graceful way to say it. I lost my dough.

"Congratulations, Sebby," Barbie said after it was done.

"Thanks," I said, holding my stomach, scrunching my shoulder blades. The pain was gone! "Wow, I feel normal again."

"Normal? You? Never," Barbie said.

"I'm starving to death!"

"You're definitely yourself. Hey, what's that?"

A howling kind of noise came from the far end of the cavern, where we hadn't gone yet. Barbie turned the flashlight that way. It was Stupid, sitting in the darkness trying to bark like a dog. Like he wanted to show us something.

Quickly me and Barbie walked over there. Through the glasses, it looked like Stupid was in front of a black hole surrounded by swirling colors. At first I thought it was the entrance to one of those dark tunnels without any curlicue veins, but as we got closer it became clear that the black hole was made of rocks. A pile of fieldstones had been stacked to fill the tunnel opening, just like back at the henhouse.

We also saw the shape of a small white rectangle coming into focus. It turned out to be an envelope propped on a rock. And it had writing on it.

SEBBY & BARBIE

We both recognized the handwriting. Our names were written in the block letters Jed always used. He had the neatest handwriting of any guy I'd ever met. It looked like the lettering in cartoon dialogue, or in the house designs Ma would cut out of the Sunday newspaper and hang on the refrigerator to show Pa what she wanted him to build on her dream lake.

"Okay, this is one of my fantasies, isn't it," I said, and pinched myself on the arm to wake up.

"You're gonna have a bruise there tomorrow, goofaling," Barbie said.

The envelope must have been there for a while. The damp paper wilted a little in my hand. The surface felt grainy with dust.

"You gonna open it?"

I turned the envelope over and looked for a spot to slip my finger under the flap. The glue had stuck so tight in the dampness that there wasn't any place to fit my stubby finger. I had an urge to tear open the envelope, but I was afraid of ripping whatever was inside, too. I held the envelope out to Barbie. "Here, you do it. You have nails."

I held the flashlight while Barbie carefully worked a fingernail under an edge until the flap peeled up. She pulled out a piece of folded notebook paper and read the letter out loud.

DEAR SEBBY (& BARBIE IF HE DIDN'T ESCAPE YOU),

IF YOU FIND THIS NOTE, THAT MEANS YOU HAVE FOUND THE WALL BEHIND THE HENHOUSE THAT GRAMPA OR SOMEONE BUILT TO KEEP PEOPLE OUT OF THIS PLACE. GO BACK HOME AND NEVER COME INTO THESE CAVES AGAIN! DO NOT, I REPEAT, DO NOT GO BEYOND THIS POINT. YOU WILL BE SORRY. BELIEVE ME, I AM. MAYBE SOMEDAY I'LL BE ABLE TO TELL YOU ABOUT IT. I HOPE SO. BUT UNTIL THAT DAY COMES, YOU'RE JUST GOING TO HAVE TO LISTEN TO ME. ARE YOU LISTENING? I MEAN IT, YOU TWO! PUT THE ROCKS BACK WHERE YOU FOUND THEM, BOARD UP THE STORAGE CLOSET IN THE HENHOUSE, AND FORGET YOU EVER FOUND THIS PLACE. YOUR LIFE MAY DEPEND ON IT.

LOVE,
YOUR BROTHER,
JED

∽ 13 ∾

I couldn't stop turning the flashlight to look at the looming wall of stones, and Barbie had to keep grabbing my arm to see the paper. By the time she got to the end of Jed's letter, Barbie was practically hyperventilating. I couldn't tell whether she was terrified or excited. Maybe she was both. I sure was, to see what was on the other side of that wall. I inched my fingers around the smallest rock in front of our faces, trying to make a window.

"Duh, Seb, didn't you hear what Jed said?"

"Yeah, he said not to go beyond the wall. He didn't say anything about just looking."

"Oh . . . true," she said. "But those stones are packed too tight to move any from the middle. We'll have to take them from the top." Which was out of our reach. So I got down on all fours to become a scaffold, with the flashlight propped beside me like a spotlight. Barbie climbed up on my back, and pretty soon the first rock hit the ground. It made plain white sparks and a big CLUNK!

While she worked, I thought out loud. "He must've meant Grampa built the *other* wall to keep people out. Jed must've built this one to keep us away from wherever the tunnel goes. Then he left the letter, went out through the henhouse, and replaced that wall to seal the tunnel before he ran away."

Barbie paused, with a big rock in her hands, I guessed from the weight of her. "Unless he sneaked back and did it recently."

"After he ran away? You think Jed has been back home? And are you gonna drop that rock or are you trying to break my back?"

"I dunno, just an idea." Barbie tossed the rock. "Okay, I think I'll be able to see out now."

I craned my neck to watch her poke her head out through the opening. I could see her silhouette even though the flashlight had fallen down and was glowing straight into a stone. That meant—

"Hey, there's light on the other side, isn't there?"

"Yeah, a sunbeam hits the ground up ahead a bit."

I shimmied to shrug Barbie off my back. "Get down, Shish, I wanna see."

She jumped off me, and I climbed up onto some rocks she'd thrown on the floor. While poking my head out through the opening I remembered something else and turtled back inside. "Thanks," I said, grabbing the magic glasses off the top of Barbie's head.

"Wish I'd thought of that. Now what do you see?"

"The blinking colors aren't all over the place like in the cavern, but they do run along the tunnel in veins like we saw on the way down," I told her. Then I couldn't help it, I had to tear away more rocks.

"Uh, Seb? Supper is *that* way." She pointed backwards.

"Don't you want to find out what happened to Jed?"

I expected her to say, "What part of 'Do Not, I Repeat, Do Not Go Beyond This Point' do you not understand," but she surprised me by climbing up next to me and helping to widen the opening. "It can't hurt if we go a little farther and see where that daylight is coming from, can it?" she said. "I mean, it doesn't look any more dangerous than what we've already been through. And Jed lived to tell about it. Or will someday."

In a few minutes we had cleared a big enough hole in the wall to climb through. Breathless with effort, trembling with nervousness, we crept along. We didn't know what to be careful about, but we were being careful.

As we got closer to the sunbeam, our eyes adjusted and we could see each gray lump in the walls. We turned off the tired flashlight to save the last of the batteries.

The crack of daylight grew longer and wider as we approached along the curving tunnel. Then there was a boulder to squeeze around. I squeezed first—and felt the ground give way underfoot as I stepped out into broad daylight. Dirt slid against dirt. A terrifying noise.

"Whoa, Barbie! Stop!" I screamed, reaching to grab her. One more step forward and I'd have gone over the crumbling edge. She pulled me toward her, my heart beating in my ears. I caught my breath, and then from the crack at the edge of the boulder we carefully looked out.

We had reached the end of the mountain, what was left of it. The beginning of the gore. Only that boulder stood between us and a long fall.

We looked down on a huge mossy green circle that could have passed for something natural if it wasn't squatting in an unnatural churned up piece of ground.

Odum's Onion. ORC.

"Oh! Jed!" Barbie said in gasps.

All of a sudden I was more worried about my brother than I could ever put into words. Because instantly I realized it probably wasn't Pa he'd run away from after all. It probably had something to do with this place.

Had he fallen off the cliff and gotten hurt? But who would have found him? And why wouldn't he have come home after that? Where was he now, and where was he calling from on those nights when the phone rang once?

In silence me and Barbie stood clinging to the boulder, staring out over the gore. From here it looked even more bare and miserable than from Kettle Ridge. At least over there you could turn your head the other way and see the land the way it ought to be. Kettle Ridge was a long way from here, a hazy line in the distance. All the land in between used to be connected, rolling hills and valleys, but Odum's bulldozers had scooped out the triangle. There was just one small spot of green in sight, a natural ravine tucked between slag piles and bumping up against the cliff near the narrow point of the mine wedge. My Hole in the Wall.

"Look there!" Barbie said, pointing to it. "Some kind of park! People who work for ORC must go there during their breaks."

"No, nobody goes there," I said. "It's really out of the way. It just looks close to ORC from up here."

"How do you know that?" She stared at me. I looked away. "Never mind, I can guess," she said. "That's where you disappear to all the time when Ma's trying to get you to do your homework, isn't it." I shrugged. I knew I was busted, but after all we'd been through today, I didn't care anymore. If she wanted to go to my hideout, I'd take her.

And then she had to go and yank on my arm, trying to drag me back the way we came. "Hurry up, Seb. We gotta go tell Ma. She can get the police to collect all the evidence and find out what happened to Jed!"

I would have wrung myself free, except I was afraid I'd spin off in the wrong direction and fall off the edge of the world. But I did dig in my heels so she couldn't drag me another inch.

Oh, cheese, there went my toes, right through the tips of my sneakers.

"Just what do you plan to tell Ma?" I said.

"Everything! She has a right to know what's on her own property, Seb."

"She also has a right to ground us forever when she finds out *everything*. Do you really wanna be stuck in the house when we could be out looking for Jed?"

"Let's just follow the rules, okay? Let the adults handle it. In case you didn't notice, Sebby, we're just kids. We can't do anything."

"Oh, yeah? That's what you think. I mean, well, I may be just a kid, but"—I pointed the ol' Daniels eyebrow in the direction of the gore—"I happen to know my way around this place. And believe me, nobody who follows the rules is gonna find out any of Boots Odum's secrets. After we know something for certain about Jed, then we can tell Ma. I promise."

Barbie finally let go of my aching elbow and crossed her arms to stare me down. "Okay, what do you have in mind?"

I was glad she said that, because if she hadn't I was gonna hafta try and bend back her wrist. If I could get her on her knees, I could make her do anything. Unfortunately, there was also the risk of missing her wrist and getting my *blankety-blank* kicked.

"Well . . . ," I said, "we don't want Ma coming to look for us. So . . . the first thing," I said (making it up as I went), "is to get home in time for spaghetti night, or there won't be a second thing."

We hurried home, talking it over on the way. We'd return to the cavern after supper, we decided, and bring the rest of the chickens so whatever was petrifying them could leave their bodies. Ma would never even have to know what had happened to them. Sweet! And we'd board up the hole in the feed closet so the hens couldn't get out again. Something back there had to have caused the petrifying problem, we figured.

We'd get fresh batteries for the flashlight tomorrow so we could look around for more clues in the tunnel and cavern. And then we'd sneak into the gore to look around at the base of the cliff below the tunnel. If there was any sign of Jed in sight, we'd find it.

Along our walk home we came across Celery sitting on a rock, shivering. She fluttered onto my sneaker and rode the rest of the way back to the henhouse. Barney was thrilled to see her. I propped Jed's protest signs against the hole in the closet to keep Celery out of there during supper time.

We had no idea what hour it was, so we hurried into the house. Grum sat in her rocker, clicking her false teeth over her yarn ball. Ma hunched over the sink clanking pots and pans. The pillow and the cushions on the couch looked as if Pa had just gotten up. Everything seemed normal. The tunnel, the cavern, the rock wall, the boulder—none of that seemed real. Not the visit from Odum, not Ma's fight with Pa, not him leaving.

Maybe none of that had happened. Maybe I'd imagined all of it. The whole day. No, three whole days! Maybe I'd just now gotten out of bed Thursday morning and was on my way to tend the chickens. They'll all gather around my feet when I walk in, squawking for their corn.

"Good, just in time to wash your hands for supper," said Ma with a smile over her shoulder. Her glasses were all fogged up with steam, making me think of the magic glasses that had shown us the secret world hidden in the rocks. I felt in my pocket for them, and instead something crinkled under my hand. Jed's letter. Just as good. It proved the chaos was all real.

Humming, Ma turned to stir something on the stove. And then the hum broke right out into an old rock 'n roll song. Not a sad sort of my-life's-gone-wrong song, either. A dancing-in-the-streets sort of song. You'd think she'd be in a sad mood after what happened with Pa, not knowing what the future would be, but I hadn't seen her looking this happy in a long time. No, I'd never seen her looking this happy. She looked younger and perkier, as if weights had been lifted off her face.

Barbie and I made faces at each other. I shrugged. She shrugged back. Then we smiled, just happy to see Ma happy.

Grum looked up and smiled at us smiling at each other. "So, what have you two been up to?" She always wanted to know that.

"Oh, not much. Just goofing around outside," I said. "What have you two been up to?"

"Let's see. Your mother and I rented a family movie for tonight, then we both had a little nap, and now I'm keeping her company while she makes supper."

"Cool," I said, mostly about the family movie. We hadn't watched one in months. Pa never liked the ones Ma let us kids watch, and he'd get all ornery if we cut into his time with the remote control, so we just gave up and did other things.

While Ma pulled the garlic bread out of the oven, Barbie reached the plates down from the cupboard and handed them to me. I set them on the table without bribery or blackmail.

Now Ma looked at me suspiciously. Or maybe it was just concern. "Hey, Seb, how's that stomachache of yours? I was thinking, maybe we should take you to the walk-in clinic in Exton tomorrow. They're open Sundays, and they take the government insurance for kids. Grum says if there's a big copay, we can sell some cuckoo clocks."

"That's right, we can," Grum chimed her agreement. She had just made herself comfortable on the couch with her feet up on Pa's pillow and was channel surfing the home shopping stations. "Some things are more important than keepsakes. On Monday we'll ride to Exton to sell them and stop on the way home to get Sebby some good sneakers."

I was really touched. "Thanks, Grum, but you don't have to sell any clocks. Well, maybe one, for sneakers, if you really want to, but not for doctor bills because guess what? My cookie dough came up a few minutes ago!" I announced this with a flourish of the forks I was setting on the table. "Ma, I hope you made a lot of food."

It was typical Saturday night spaghetti, Ma style. She'd boiled the noodles to death and burned the sauce. The meat-balls were tiny hard lumps of beef that made my molars ache, with so many chunky onions in them that I started burping before I was even done eating. Best meal of my life.

After we got done cleaning up, it was already getting dark outside. Barbie and I grabbed our sweatshirts and headed for the door to rescue Barney's harem and block off the tunnel.

"Where do you two think you're going at this hour?" said Ma, squatting in front of the DVD player. "Don't you want to watch the movie?"

Me and Barbie winced at each other. The disappointment in Ma's voice was painful to hear. My stomach swam with a feeling I knew well, guilt.

"Of course we want to, Ma," said Barbie. "We just forgot you had a movie, that's all."

"That's right. We can . . . *play outside* tomorrow," I said more to Barbie than to Ma.

"Kids don't play outside like they used to," Grum said.

She sat with her string in her rocker while Barbie and I

cuddled with Ma on the couch. I felt warm and safe and, for the first time in a long time, like everything was going to be all right.

And then, when the movie was almost over, the phone rang. I felt Ma stiffen as we waited, hoping not to hear another ring so we'd know it was Jed, letting us know he was okay.

It rang again, and a third time. Who could be calling at this hour? A call this late could never be good.

"Sebby, will you get that?" Ma said, since I was on the kitchen side of the cuddle.

I didn't want to get the phone. I was afraid it would be Pa calling to ruin the good mood everyone was in. But Ma asked me to, so I answered it, cautiously. "Hello?"

"Sebby, good, it's you. Listen, I don't have much time. Don't let anyone else know it's me."

It was Jed! "What's wrong?" I whispered into the phone. Something in his voice made me picture him looking over his shoulder, but I couldn't imagine what he was afraid of seeing. I looked over my shoulder into the living room. They had paused the movie and the three of them were talking about something that had just happened.

"Things have gone too far," Jed said. "As long as you have that cookie dough in you, you can't stay home. Get off the property or who knows . . ."

"But—"

"Look, I can't explain. Just do as I say." And click. He hung up.

"Who was it?" Ma asked.

"Oh, just a courtesy call." I smiled to myself. That should do it.

"How rude!" said Grum. "Up is down and war is peace, too. Those telemarketers . . ."

That night I was so tired, I don't even remember going upstairs. I just remember waking up in the dark not knowing where I was, with my bunk shaking, my back aching, and an awful noise filling my head. It was Barbie having one of her nightmare howls, and Ma trying to shake her out of it.

"Barbie, wake up, honey."

"Where's Pa!" Actual words. She was awake now.

"He's not here. Don't worry, it was just a dream," Ma soothed. "You can go back to sleep."

Maybe she could, but now I couldn't. I lay there thinking about everything: Celery, the other chickens, the secret tunnel, Pa, Boots Odum, Jed. Especially Jed. How did he know about the cookie dough? He must still be around Kokadjo! And why did he warn me? He didn't give me a chance to tell him I'd heaved. Was I still in danger? Should I still get off the property, like he said? Maybe spend the night at the Hole in the Wall? But if our property was dangerous, the gore probably wasn't any safer. Maybe I should sneak into one of the outbuildings up at the commune. There were plenty of places to hide up there.

And then I realized. Of course! The answer had been right under my nose the whole time. Or right next door. Zensylvania. Where if you sat in the right tree with a pair of binoculars on a clear day, you could see in our kitchen window. That's where Jed must be. And as soon as I knew everyone had fallen back to sleep, I was going to ride my bike up there and find him.

☙ 14 ❧

I would have gone to find Jed right then if it hadn't been for Grum's cuckoos. They all chose that moment to go off, the one in her bedroom and all of them out in Jed's castle. Everyone in the house was so startled, we added screams to the noise. Good thing Pa wasn't there.

We waited a minute for the cuckoos to get past the hour and quiet down, but it was a minute without end. Grum's bed creaked and the light showed under her door. She was up fiddling with the cuckoo in her room. It stopped, but the ones in Jed's castle kept going and going.

"Someone's been fooling with those clocks again!" Grum called.

"Not it," I said.

"Me neither," Barbie said.

Grum knew that me and Barbie used to have fun playing with the cuckoos when Jed first moved out to the castle. We'd set the pendulums all out of sync, and after a while they'd all sing together. "Like magic," Barbie said.

"No, they synchronize because their motions send perturbations through the walls," Jed said. I asked him if that was anything like ESP, and he said he wouldn't be surprised if the same theory applied, but he meant that they vibrated themselves into unison. I sure missed listening to Jed. But with any luck I'd be hearing his voice again real soon.

"Sebby," Ma called in a groggy voice, "go do something about that racket."

And then I had a thought that scared the idea of going to Zensylvania straight out of my head. "Ma, what if someone's out there?"

The light in her room came on. She appeared in the doorway tying her robe, her hair sticking out all over and night cream splotched on her face. "Seb, where's your baseball bat?"

"Uh . . . Yankee Stadium?" Which in my imagination was located across the road in a certain cave where Babe Ruth hung out with outfielders from another galaxy.

"Never mind." Ma went back in her room and emerged with Pa's hunting rifle. "You kids stay here with Grum. Lock yourselves in her room till I get back."

Grum appeared in her doorway looking skeptical. "Claire, is that thing loaded?"

"Well, I, ah, don't know," Ma admitted. She didn't like guns. She didn't even know how to use one.

"Find me some bullets, then. I'm going with you." Grum held her hand out for the gun. She was a good shot. When she lived in the gore she used to pick squirrels off the bird feeder from her bedroom window.

"Sweet," I said, jumping down from the bunk. "I'm going too. Ow!" Upon landing a sharp pain ran up through my backbone.

"Next time use the ladder," Ma said, handing Grum the bullets.

"I'm not staying here alone," Barbie said. The two of us helped Grum into her shoes, then held her loose-skinned arms as she picked her way down the stairs. Usually Grum only did the stairs once in the morning and once at night because they were hard on her knees.

She stopped in front of the mirror to pluck her new perm into place.

I yanked the door open. It had been raining again, probably pouring, as I immediately felt when I stepped onto the so-called lawn. Luckily I was barefoot or what was left of my sneakers would have dissolved. An inch of water had pooled all around. And here's the really strange part: that green stuff which passed for grass had turned all hard and pokey like a welcome mat made of Velcro. Don't things usually get soft when they're soaked in water? Anyway, I didn't have a good feeling about Grum walking in this. The rutty lane was dangerous enough in the daylight when the ground was dry.

"Grum, it's really nasty out here. You should go back in. I can take the gun. Pa taught me to shoot." It wasn't a lie, exactly. He had let me aim the gun at a beer can once when he was target practicing.

My grandmother hesitated, clinging to the railing, and craned her neck out toward the cuckoo ruckus. The porch light made a moony glow around her white asbestos curls, and without her teeth in, her cheeks looked like sinkholes in the strip mine. She could have been some photographer's masterpiece.

"I'll pray for Jesus to guide me," I offered. If anything would convince her to turn back, that would. But no, she was too worried to leave it to me to leave it to Jesus.

"You two each take an elbow and help her," Ma said. "I'll light your way—I've got the flashlight. Oh, my, we need to get some new batteries. That trip to the commune must have used these up."

"Yeah, it must have," I said.

And so we headed out slowly, taking careful steps. There weren't any lights on in Jed's castle. The farther we got away from the house, the darker the ground seemed. The dying flashlight cast a weak yellow arc on the puddles and rivulets we steered around.

"Ow!" My bare toe knocked something. It didn't hurt, though, just startled me.

Ma snapped the flashlight that way, and it spotlighted the cat dish, tipped on its side and spilling milk. "Who's still wasting our good milk on the cat!"

"Who might that be?" said Grum, pointing the gun at two foot-long shadows. Shoes, to be specific. Ma turned the thin beam on them to reveal a man's body sprawled toes-up between the henhouse and Jed's castle.

Ma swore at Pa. They were his shoes.

She traced the light along the rest of him. Yep, his best pants, his dress shirt, and his face, too. What we could see of it. Because on top of his chest sat Stupid, purring like Pa was his best friend. I was amazed. Pa the cat-hater had been taking care of Fluffy Kitty!

"That's my boy," Grum said in mock pride. She clucked and gave Pa a poke with the gun. "Wake up, Sleeping Beauty." The cat meowed and ran toward the henhouse.

I would have checked to see if Pa was still breathing, but he started snoring when Grum poked him. He was passed out drunk, or so I figured from the sour beer smell. Luckily he'd fallen face up instead of down, or he could have drowned in the mud puddle. Or unluckily! Wishing Pa dead flooded me with pleasure. And then guilt.

The cuckoos were still at it, so we left Pa and carefully made our way out to Jed's castle. The nonstop cuckoo riot made me feel so crazy, I itched to run ahead and stop the clocks. For once I kind of understood the feeling Pa must have had when he used to go to such lengths shutting them up.

But I held myself back to let Grum lean on me. Even though it wasn't far, it took a long time for Grum to find firm ground to put her weight on. Between steps I wiggled my toes in the nubby mud.

When Ma opened the door, a mixture of smells wafted out. Candles, sour beer, and something sweet that I had been smelling a lot of lately—the Perfume-Lady smell in the cookie dough and the secret tunnel. Barbie glanced nervously at me, and I knew she recognized it too.

Back when he moved to the castle, Jed had run an extension cord from the house for electricity. Pa had yanked that out of the outlet with some flaming words after Jed ran away, so now our only light was a flashlight fading fast. Grum lowered herself onto the bed to rest under the crazy cuckoos as Ma shone the narrowing beam around to find some candles and matches.

There they were, on a milk crate beside Jed's bed, along with a bunch of empty beer cans. Pa must have been here earlier tonight drowning his sorrows with the cuckoos!

The candles soon filled the little room with flickering light, and we saw the birds all popping out and singing. Grum reached up carefully to remove a clock from the Sheetrock wall.

I remembered when we'd put up those walls, Jed and me and Pa, the day after Jed got the idea to move out there with Grum's clocks. Until then, the play castle had just had bare stone walls. The clocks needed a flat surface to hang on, and a new layer of insulation in between would keep the room warm in winter.

Pa whistled and told growing-up-in-the-gore stories as he showed me and Jed how to spread the Sheetrock mud over the seams and sand it down smooth. That day was the last time I remembered seeing those two in the same room for more than ten minutes without getting at each other's throats.

Now picturing Pa all pathetic in the mud with Jed's cat made me feel bad for him. He blamed himself for Jed running away. We all blamed Pa. But maybe we were all wrong. That note Jed had left in the caves made me wonder. I wished I could figure out the truth. But first, quiet the birds.

When Grum took down the first clock, its cuckoo stopped singing, but the others kept at it. Grum inspected the clock front and back, then put it back on the wall. The cuckoo started popping in and out again.

Barbie took another clock down. The cuckoo stopped. She put the clock back and the bird resumed its cuckoo business.

I gave it a try—same thing. On off, on off, on off. It was pretty cool. I wasn't minding the noise so much now.

"Oh, for heaven's sake, enough of that!" Ma started taking the clocks down and piling them on the bed. We all helped. The room gradually grew quiet. Outside the cat meowed.

Grum wagged her head like a pendulum itself. "I don't understand," she said. "This cuckoo madness isn't even possible."

"It has to be possible," I said. "It's happening."

"Maybe Pa did something to jam the clocks?" suggested Barbie. "Like he used to when he was a kid."

"Except in reverse," I said.

Grum continued shaking her head. "Even Craig couldn't cause this chaos. Pendulums work because of gravity. They follow predictable rules. The clocks should sound the hour, and that's it—and then only if the weights on the chains have been reset. None of these clocks have been wound up!"

"Okay, that's eerie," Ma said. "But they're quiet now. What do you say we go back to bed and figure this out tomorrow?"

Grum nodded. "It's been a long day."

She didn't know the half of it.

On our way past Pa, Barbie said, "Shouldn't we bring him inside?"

Ma looked at him with an expression alternating between pity and anger, but leaning toward pity. Stepping toward him she said, "Sebby, he's heavy. You'll have to help me." Man, he looked ridiculous lying there with his arms flopped out to the sides like a cheerleader.

"No!" Grum said sharply. "You told Craig what needed to be said, Claire, and now what he needs from you is tough love. Leave him be. He's made his own bed, let him lie in it."

"A water bed," I almost said, but Grum wouldn't have appreciated me joking when she was being serious.

At that the rest of us went to lie in our soft, comfortable beds.

The next morning I woke up before Barney. My back was killing me. Plus I needed to use the bathroom. And since I had to go downstairs anyway, I figured I'd put on what was left of my sneakers and drop by Zensylvania to corner Jed. During the cuckoo snafu I'd forgotten that plan, but now it was the first thing on my mind. After a bowl of Cheerios.

I was tipping the bowl to drink the thick sugar milk out of it when I noticed the trail of dried mud across the linoleum. The mud tracked into the living room and stopped at the top of a head. Pa's.

Someone had dragged him in after all, his feet pointing toward the couch. He lay sprawled face-up in the same posture we'd seen him in last night, right down to the cheerleader arms. Except for the slight motion of his chest as he breathed, he looked stone still. He wasn't even snoring. From the looks of it, he still hadn't woken up from when he passed out, and I didn't want to be the first person he saw when he opened his bloodshot eyes. I took off.

The drag marks came up the steps. Pa's heavy body had

left a deep trench in the mud. Foot trails had dried in front of the stairs, continuing out behind the house from when we'd gone to check the cuckoos. The footprints had hardened like you see sometimes in concrete sidewalks. Like fossils! Grum's shoe fossils wobbled at the edges, showing how careful she was to find a firm grip. Barbie and I had both been barefoot. Barbie's big toes stuck out of the prints like fat heads. I filed it away for teasing later.

Who had brought Pa inside? I tried walking in the half-erased tracks under the drag marks to identify them. They couldn't be mine—I'd been sleeping. They couldn't be Grum's because Grum couldn't drag Pa into the house without winding up in an ambulance. The prints looked longer than Ma's feet, more like Pa's. But Pa couldn't have dragged himself. It must have been Barbie, even though I didn't see any fathead toes. She was the one who'd suggested bringing him inside in the first place. Her feet were the one part of her that I hadn't outgrown this week. Oh, and her fingernails.

Now that it was daylight and I had followed the foot fossils most of the way there already, I thought I'd look inside Jed's castle. Maybe I'd find some kind of clue there that we'd missed the first million times we searched. After he didn't come home, Ma had checked all of Jed's pockets while me and Barbie rifled through his books and papers hunting for names, phone numbers, anything that might give us a lead. We contacted all his friends from school, all his old girlfriends, even a bunch of people he knew from marches, protests, rallies, and such. Nobody had seen or heard a trace of him.

Upon opening the door, the sweet smell inside the castle hit me again, but I was hit harder by the sight of the empty wall where the cuckoos had hung. It used to be just plain, grayish-white Sheetrock with white stripes of joint compound because Jed didn't want to take the time to paint before moving in. Well, not anymore. Now it had an intricate design, all beautiful swoops and swirls of pastel colors, just faint enough that we wouldn't have noticed it last night in the candlelight. The pattern looked a little like the baby blankets Grum crocheted. No, more like seashells all tossed together, or a bunch of old jewelry spread out on a satin sheet. Then I realized exactly what it reminded me of: the art in Boots Odum's house. His paintings.

Had he come out here and painted Jed's wall? No, of course not.

Had Jed come back and done it? If so, it had to be after Thursday morning when Stupid showed up inside the henhouse. I'd have noticed the change when I checked the castle then. Was the paint still wet? I ran my finger along the seashell curves, and that's when I realized something that made the hair stand up on the back of my neck.

There wasn't any paint on the drywall. The color came from *underneath* the layer of unpainted paper. It had an almost shimmering lifelike quality to it. And as I ran my finger over it, the color began to move. I didn't need any magic glasses to see it.

I yelped. Because now I knew exactly what it was. That *stuff*. Whatever it was in the rocks that made the amazing colors. It had somehow leached into the wall. And somehow set the cuckoos off. And who knew what else it could somehow do? Straighten Miss Beverly's neck . . . and turn her prized poodle into a statue.

Was that *stuff* what Jed had tried to warn me and Barbie about? Only one way to know, and that was to find him. Which I'd planned to do in the first place, before I got distracted. If only my brain could be more like Barbie's sock drawer.

I went running out of the castle straight to my bike and was rounding the corner of the house when I had to slam on the brakes. Or else run over Barbie. Whoops, we had a plan to take all those poor petrified chickens with their pathetic eyes to the cavern and return them to their feathers before breakfast.

"Where do you think you're going?" Barbie asked. A common question around me.

"Oh, just goofing around on my bike while waiting for Barbie Big Toes to get out of bed." To prove it I hopped my bike along one of the grooves in the hardened mud.

Barbie shook her head at me. "I'm *sooooo* glad we're not identical. Anyway, Mr. No, why did you go and drag Pa inside last night after what Grum said?"

"Who, me? I thought you did it." The shock made me fall off my bike. Groan, groan, my aching back. I must have slept on it wrong. No, wait, Barbie stood on it wrong with those heavy rocks yesterday. No wonder my back killed.

"I didn't do it. And Ma says she didn't do it. So who did it?"

"Maybe one of his drinking buddies?"

Barbie nodded. "Makes sense. We'd better hurry—there's just enough time to save the chickens before we have to get ready for church."

Our plan was to load up the wheelbarrow and the little red wagon with all the chickens and haul them to the cavern in one trip. Celery came fluttering to sit on my sneaker the moment I walked inside the henhouse. "Ahoy, mate," I said, petting her head as Barbie opened the closet.

But Barbie was the one who swore like a parrot. "Someone's been in here!"

My perfect sister, swearing? I never heard of such a thing. "This can't be good." I ran to see.

All the stuff had been neatly put away on the shelves. We pulled down the things in front of the hidden door only to see that the barn boards had been replaced by a big piece of plywood. Nails with broad heads had been spiked into the studs an inch apart. That plywood wasn't going to come off without a lot of work.

"Pa must have done this last night, before he . . . you know!" I said.

"I guess so. But where did he put the chickens? I hope he didn't just leave them where they were!"

Me and Barbie looked at each other, then tore around the corner to search the coop. There all the hens were, right where they belonged: sitting on their nests like sculptures on display.

"Whoever did this has a sick sense of humor," Barbie said.

I went along the rows and waved my hand in front of their eyes, which moved. "They're still alive!"

"How will we get the sick hens to that cavern now?" Barbie said.

"Maybe we can find a place to squeeze in between the wall and the cliff behind the coop?" I said.

Barbie nodded, but doubtfully. "Maybe, if we can clip away some vines."

We went out to look. Celery didn't want to let go my foot so she went along for the ride.

This time Barbie and I both cussed like parrots at what we saw. Someone had wedged rocks into the gap between the building and the mountain. Mortar oozed out between the stones. It was still damp to the touch. My heart felt like a balloon with all the air gone out of it. How were we going to save the chickens now?

ೞ 15 ೞ

We went back inside the coop to talk it over. I sat in the wheelbarrow with my soul mate in my lap and pet her head forlornly. "I'm sorry, Celery. I'd love to save your aunties. I really would." I felt worse than I had when we found the chickens petrified to begin with. At least then I thought they were dead and didn't have any reason to hope. Now I knew they were alive, and could be saved, if only we could get them to the cavern.

"There has to be another way," Barbie said.

"Because where there's a will, there's a—" I said, mimicking Grum's voice, and then it came to me: "A ladder! We can take Pa's extension ladder into the gore and climb up to the tunnel from there."

Barbie wasn't having that. "Oh, Sebby. Bad idea. Even if Ma and Grum didn't catch us trying to drag that heavy ladder and all those chickens over there, the goons would. Plus it would be suicidal trying to climb up all that loose dirt. But another entrance is a good thought. Those tunnels probably have other ways in. Remember all those passages that went off to the left?"

"Yeah, off to the left . . . that would be down . . . no, up—" I crossed my eyes, thinking.

"Toward the commune!" Barbie realized. "Too bad Cluster's gone. We could ask her if she knows of any caves back there that we could try. It could take us days to find an entrance on our own. And then, more days to find our way to the cavern. If there's even a way at all."

She was pretty right, because me and Grum's binoculars hadn't spotted any caves when we were on our Zensylvania reconnaissance missions. But then again, we were more focused on windows than holes in the ground. Anyway, I had another idea.

"There may be someone else up in Zensylvania who can help us," I said, excitedly, since it would allow me to kill two birds with one stone, as Grum would say. Although really we were trying to keep the birds alive. "Jed."

"Jed? At the commune? You mean, like, now?"

"Yeah, still," I said, and then explained in a big long sentence with no breath (so Barbie wouldn't have a chance to cut me off) the reasons why I thought he'd been living there all this time. "So, we should go up there right now, find him, and have him explain what the heck."

And then in her own big long sentence of revenge Barbie talked me out of my idea because if our runaway brother had been living at the commune all this time, wouldn't A) Cluster have let it slip to us, or B) Jed have moved away with the rest of the commune, or C) he have at the very least gotten out of there before Odum's goons fenced him in?

"What do you mean, fence?" I said.

"The fence they already had half built yesterday afternoon. Don't you remember us talking about it on the way to skating? How, like, dozens of goons were up on Kettle Ridge cutting branches and unrolling this thick wire mesh all around the tree trunks at the edge of the property?"

Uh, no. I vaguely remembered voices buzzing in the SUV, and one of them might possibly have been mine, but the major thing I remembered from that ride was hiding my petrified pet chick and planning how I was going to explain it to Barbie.

Yesterday afternoon seemed like a long time ago now.

"Oh, yeah, good point about the fence," I said, taking her word for it. "But where else could Jed have been to know about that cookie dough in my guts? Can you answer me that?"

Barbie thought a moment, slowly turned, and pointed toward the boarded up feed closet.

I banged my hand on my head. Why didn't I think of it first? "Of course! He's been living in the tunnels this whole time!"

"Well, not necessarily. He could be living anywhere, but if he knows other entrances to the tunnels, he could easily sneak back here to keep an eye on us. Or an ear."

"So to save the chickens, we have to find Jed."

"Fat chance of that! No, we have to find another entrance to the tunnels. C'mon, Seb, when you and your spaceship brain are out exploring, have you ever seen another cave nearby?"

That question did it. Duh! Of course I'd seen another cave. Many a time. It didn't lead to the tunnel where Celery got her life back, but it might work the same magic. It was in the same chunk of mountain.

So I told Barbie about the Hole in the Wall, and we decided to take the petrified hens there. We had to do *something* with those chickens, whether or not we could save them. We couldn't just leave them sitting on their nests with their pathetic eyes and let Ma find them like that. She already thought Odum had kidnapped them anyway, so why not take them to the gore to live? (Or not.)

But first we had to suffer through the weekly butt torture better known as church. There was no getting out of it with the Ma and Grum tag-team ironing the dress pants and pointing to the shower. It was only an hour of sitting on the hard pew but it felt like eternity on my aching back. Slouching usually made it better, but that day it only made the pain worse. So did jiggling.

"It's all the jiggling you do that makes your butt hurt," Jed once told me. "Resistance is futile. You might as well sit still." This was easy for him to say. After he started high school, Ma let him choose whether he wanted to go to church anymore, and he chose to sleep in.

Anyway, I tried his advice and sat straight up without jiggling. It made Barbie seem awfully short all of a sudden. But the hour lasted just as long as ever.

My teacher said hello in the vestibule after the sermon. Ms. Byron goes to the same church we do. Pa had been surprised to hear that a kneejerk liberal feminazi even went to church. Funny, I didn't see *him* there.

"Why, Sebastian, I think you've grown six inches since Friday," Ms. Byron said. Her eyebrows nearly hit her Sunday hat.

"Only three inches," Barbie said.

"He's finally decided to listen to his old grandmother and stand up straight," Grum said proudly. "Praise the Lord."

As we crossed Kettle Ridge on the way home, I couldn't resist staring out at the gore, as usual. Barbie craned her neck to look out my side, too, squinting with her hand over her eyes. Remembering yesterday, I scanned the faraway cliff on the narrow end, looking for the tunnel we'd nearly fallen out of, but it just blended into the mass of endless grayness. The boulder in its mouth probably made the tunnel impossible to see from the outside anyway.

A motion in the middle of the stripped area caught my eye, though. A silver car on Odum's Gash. And a black one. And a red truck. A whole scattering of vehicles, heading in. You could see them blipping between the slag piles. Barbie leaned closer. She practically climbed on my lap, pressing her nose against the window.

"What do you see?" I said, resisting the urge to shove her back over to her own seat. We were nearing the edge of the kettle top now and would soon lose the view.

"What do you see?" Ma echoed, looking at us through the rear-view mirror. The SUV made the turn down the hill, and the road weaved through pines intertwined with viney shrubs.

Barbie punched my arm. I guess I shouldn't have said that. "Oh, just some cars in the gore," she answered Ma.

"That's unusual for a Sunday," said Ma. True. ORC never saw much activity on the weekends. Just a goon here and there, changing guard shifts, and Boots Odum himself went in sometimes to check on things. Most of the employees had weekends off and never went near the place until Monday morning.

"They must be godless heathens," said Grum.

Ma laughed but said, "Now now. Judge not lest ye be judged."

They had themselves a fine time exchanging Bible verses the rest of the way home, and I kept thinking about Jed. If Barbie had been right, if he'd been keeping an eye on us from the tunnels, he could be living way over on the other side of the mountain behind us. Those tunnels could go for miles and miles.

We made the turn past Ma's sign:

SORRY, NO EGGS

and instantly I realized what Barbie had been gawking at in the gore. That was Pa's truck I'd seen blipping between slag piles! It had been in the driveway when we left, but not now.

"How did Pa get past the security gate at ORC?" I whispered in Barbie's ear as we walked to the house. "Do you think he finally got himself a job there?"

"Seb, it's Sunday. He has no reason whatsoever to be at ORC."

She had a really good point. That couldn't have been Pa. "Don't worry, Shish, there are lots of red trucks in the world. Pa's probably over at the Do-Drop-Inn as usual."

"Probably," Barbie said. But she didn't sound convinced.

I barely tasted the weekly Crock-Pot roast and potatoes we had after church, I ate so fast. Barbie was shoveling the food in too. We were in a hurry to get going. Besides, swallowing without chewing made the food less painful. And that wasn't a joke about Ma's cooking. I felt like I had four hundred new molars.

"All right," said Ma the second I took my plate to the sink, "it's Sunday afternoon and I haven't seen anybody named Sebby doing any homework all weekend."

"I was planning on getting that done tonight," I said. Assuming Barbie would tell me the assignments. While my classmates had copied them into their agendas on Friday, cartoon superheroes jumped out of my pencil. Don't blame me. I am weak and superheroes are strong.

"You were, were you?" said Ma. "I was planning on your getting that done this afternoon."

"Jeez, Ma, it's not your homework! Pa's gone one day and now you want to tell me what to do every minute!"

Barbie put her head in her hands in despair. I guess I'd gone a little overboard.

Grum didn't say a word for once, but she didn't need to with that look on her face. She let her glasses slide down her nose and challenged Ma over the tops of them.

Ma was going to blow, I thought. But she spoke calmly and even sounded amused. "This morning in church your teacher asked me if I received the letter she mailed home last week requesting me to check and sign your homework each day. And I had to tell her that somehow her correspondence had escaped my notice. Now, how did that happen, Seb?"

I looked at my feet. My toes waved their sympathy.

"That's what I thought. As long as I have to sign your homework because you weren't taking responsibility for it yourself, my darling son, then, yes, I will be telling you what to do. Now sit your derriere down and get that homework done without another word of sass, or you're grounded for a week."

So I had a choice. I stared at her, squinting and biting on my lips, trying to decide what to do. It took about three seconds. "All right," I said. "I'm grounded. C'mon, Shish." And out the door I went.

"Barbie, not you? Barbie?" Ma sounded so surprised, she could barely choke the words out.

"Sorry, Ma," the Shish said, running behind me. Over her shoulder she called, "I'll make him do the homework when we get back, though. I promise!"

"Where are you two going?" Ma called out the door. I was already on my bike.

"Don't worry, Ma, we're just taking over the world!" I cackled an evil laugh as I headed up Kettle Road.

"What's this about?" Barbie huffed, pedaling hard to catch up. "I thought we decided the commune was not an option. We're supposed to be taking the hens to your Hole in the Wall."

"Decoy," I said. "We can't let her see us go into the henhouse or she'll follow us. I'd follow me if I was her."

Ma was already out in the middle of the road with her hands on her hips watching us.

"You and your big mouth," Barbie said.

"You're welcome," I said.

After we rounded a corner and Ma couldn't see us anymore, we steered off into the woods and waited there behind a pine tree until she came by in her car. Then we looped back, got the chickens we'd packed up before church, and entered the gore through the only bike-sized gap that existed in the big wall of boulders posted with shiny white AUTHORIZED PERSONNEL ONLY signs.

Barbie had stuffed a bunch of stiff hens into her school book bag, and I had loaded the rest into the large wicker backpack Pa used to carry when we went camping. Sometimes when I was really little he'd carry me in that backpack along with the bedrolls and the cans of baked beans. He'd tell the story of Jack and the Beanstalk, pretending he was the giant taking me home to eat. That was fun. Anyway, the stiff wicker felt good against my stiff back and actually made it easier to carry all that weight.

With all the unusual activity in the gore today, we had to be extra careful not to be seen. First we took the back way, cutting to the end of the first rib road, then straight across the rear of the mine to the oasis. Then we had to walk the bikes because the dirt between ribs was so loose, and in the really wet places it practically yanked us down by the feet.

"You didn't tell me we had to go through quicksand," Barbie said accusingly, as if she wouldn't have come here had she realized.

"I didn't know," I said, and it was mostly true. I knew the dirt was loose and soggy, and I was always afraid it might suck me down into the middle of the earth if I stepped wrong, but I never thought before to call it *quicksand.*

Eventually we rounded the last slag pile before the Hole

in the Wall, and my heart caught in my throat the same as always. The ravine would have been pretty anywhere, but it looked like a work of art sitting where it was. The forsythia bushes blazed yellow under the budding maples. Tucked into a hill at the back, my little hideaway stood like a wide welcoming smile. I guess that made the plywood door a big nose.

Barbie said "Oh!" behind me. "Wow. It's adorable, Seb!" She shaded her eyes and looked around, taking in the mossy clearing, the trees where squirrels chased each other, and the boulder with the dip in the middle where birds took baths. Then she lifted her eyes to scan the looming wall where bulldozers had stopped cutting away the surrounding mountain in a sheer drop. And she looked scared.

At that moment, I saw it like new myself. The cliff face had changed in the two years I'd been coming here. The trees at the top edge had gradually lost their grip on the eroding soil. Some of them had toppled over completely and were hanging upside down by their roots. A few were even clinging to life, by the looks of the green haze of buds at the ends of their limbs.

Dark jagged stripes marked the rock where water had run down and washed dirt away. Water still trickled now from yesterday's rain. The moat around my hideout had overflowed its banks with frothy colors. And now dark clouds were gathering overhead again.

"We should hurry up and do what we came for," Barbie said. "I want to get home before the storm hits."

∽ 16 ∾

We went into the cave and set down the chickens. "Nice place you have here," Barbie said, looking around approvingly.

Once you were inside, the cave got tall enough to stand up in for about the size of Jed's castle, and then it tapered down very quickly to the floor. My shelves framed the shallow edges so it felt like an attic room. I kept the stone floor swept clean and covered with a raggedy old quilt for a rug.

"So that's where that quilt went!" Barbie said. "You rotten thing. Grum accused Pa of throwing it in the garbage."

"Where do you think I found it?"

I felt in my pocket for the magic glasses. If the cave didn't swim with colors like the cavern, our plan probably wouldn't work. And I'd rather have the hens alive again, laying eggs, than spending eternity as garden statues.

"Yee-ha! Barney's gonna be a happy cock-a-doodle-dude tonight." I handed Barbie the glasses so she could see. The Hole in the Wall swam with colors, all right. If anything, the patterns shone brighter than in the big tunnel cavern. Or maybe they just seemed that way in the small space.

My back felt itchy all of a sudden. I tried to reach around and scratch myself, but I was too stiff. I stood against the wall and rubbed against the rough rock, but that made my back itch even more.

"Hey, Barbie, could you scratch my back for me? I can't reach it."

She started scratching over my shirt, but that didn't do much for me. "It feels like bugs crawling all over me. Maybe they were in the wicker pack. Can you see anything?" I yanked up my shirt.

Barbie screamed.

I screamed back.

Then I said, "Why are we screaming?"

"Sebby," she said. "You—your back. Have you looked at it in the mirror since yesterday?"

I wasn't in the habit of looking at my front in the mirror, much less my back. "No," I said. "What's wrong?" I stepped closer to the daylight and craned my neck around, trying to see what she saw, which of course only gave me a sore neck. The panicky look on Barbie's face got my heart beating faster.

"You know those colors from the paint that stuck to you in Odum's studio? Well, some of them must have sunk through your clothes! The colors are on you. They look really pale under your skin. It's like you have a tattoo!"

"But I thought you said you saw colors fly off me yesterday in the cavern!"

"I did!"

"Well, look through the glasses and tell me what you see." I handed them to her and showed her my back again.

She gasped. "Wow! The colors look really bright, and they're swirling beneath your skin. That must be what's causing the itch."

Her warm fingers made little wimpy pokes at my skin, like when she's afraid to touch something. "Your magic tattoo feels cold and hard like the bathroom floor! Does it hurt?"

"Come to think of it, yeah! My back's been killing me all day. And half the night. It's stiff. I can't move very well. I thought it was from you standing on me with rocks."

"Oh my God, Sebby! You know what this means?" She turned me around to face her. I'd never seen her so big-eyed. "You're petrified!"

"I was just thinking the same thing about you." Heh heh.

"Stop joking. I'm serious. I mean your back, Seb. It's turned to stone, like the chickens. And, yes, it scares me!"

Okay, her idea made sense, sort of, if the paint on my back was made of that stuff that petrified the eggs. Except . . . "Wait. Celery was cured in the cavern, and my cookie dough chunks came up. So why is the stuff still in my back?"

By now rain had started to sprinkle outside. We stepped deeper into the cave. Barbie shook her head. "I don't know. But we do know who might." She pointed in the direction of the ORC Onion.

"Boots Odum. Yeah. Maybe I should go show him my new tattoo! What do you bet he gives me lots of money?"

"No, Seb. You're gonna show this to *Ma*. Let her deal with him. Your life may be at stake! Do you want to wind up like Miss Beverly's poodle?"

Just then a bolt of lightning flashed outside the cave, and thunder crashed directly overhead, opening the clouds up. A sheet of rain came pouring down like a waterfall in front of the doorway, spouting inside the cave.

"We're getting flash flooded!" I said. "No way can we bike across the gore in this. I'll close the place up so we can stay dry until the storm passes over. You can light the candles." I got matches out of a coffee can and tossed them to her.

"Fine," Barbie said. "But as soon as the rain stops, we're going home and telling Ma everything. Got it?"

"Oh, all right," I said. I was pretty scared, to tell the truth. Grum would take that lightning bolt as a message from God. And it was His day. I figured I'd better pay attention.

Once I'd locked the plywood into its grooves, the rain drummed pleasantly against it, leaving us dry and cozy in the candlelight. I turned around, wiping my hands on my back pockets, and started laughing.

"Look, Barbie!"

Her book bag was jiggling. The first hen wriggled and started pecking her way out like a baby bird coming out of an egg. Barbie crawled over and loosened the strings so the others could free themselves. We laughed as the chickens came flying out of the two packs like popcorn.

Before long, the little cave was stage to a troupe of dancing chickens. But the last one still lay like a rock in the bottom of the wicker pack. I took the hen out and waved my hand back and forth before her eyes. They didn't move.

"Aw," said Barbie. "That's so sad."

I dug around in my snack stockpile and found some stale pretzels to toss to the chickens, but they jumped away like I was throwing hot coals at them. "Fine, more for me," I said, popped a pretzel in my mouth, and chomped down.

"Aaahhh!" That pretzel was harder than Ma's rock cookies. Or maybe it just felt that way to my four hundred new teeth.

I held a pretzel out to Barbie. "Sorry, they're a little stale," I said.

"No, thanks, I'm not hungry. How can you eat at a time like this? Aren't you scared?"

"Gee, no, Shish. I'm looking forward to my future as a human mood rock. Maybe I'll join the circus."

Yeah, I was scared. But I didn't want to talk about it. Or even think about it. So I pulled a bunch of blankets out of the garbage bags where I stored them and spread them out on the floor to make a mattress. "Hey, Barbie, you feel like scratching my back again?" I asked, trying to sound like I was doing her a big favor.

She scrunched her nose. "That tattoo gives me the creeps. I don't want to touch it."

"C'mon, you touched it before and it didn't kill you. It itches!"

"Oh, all right. But you have to keep your T-shirt on. Lie on your stomach."

She sat on the backs of my legs and gave my back a hard massage that felt so warm and good, I was almost asleep when the mudslide hit.

It was already noisy outside with all the thunder and pounding rain, but this was a different loud noise—a giant cracking and rolling that started above us, surrounded us, and vibrated through the ground. The candles flickered. The chickens took to the air squawking, and loose feathers rained down. Then the loud noise ended, and the normal storm noise all sounded muffled and distant, the way you can hear interstate traffic from our house during a really still moment.

"I don't have a good feeling about this." I jumped to my feet. Which sent Barbie flying backwards and complaining, but I didn't listen. I was too busy pushing and trying to pull frantically on the plywood door. I even went to the back of the cave and ran at the door to give it a flying kick. But it wasn't budging. It was bulging. And now my foot ached all the way up to my neck.

I turned to Barbie to tell her we were trapped, but the words wouldn't come out. I couldn't swallow either. I was terrified.

"Sebby, what is it? You're scaring me." Barbie ran to push and pull and kick on the door, too. And then she knew. "That noise was a mudslide. We're buried in here."

I was surprised she didn't scream. Maybe she was just too shocked. She sank down on one edge of Grum's raggedy quilt and stared at the plywood. Along the bottom and around the edges you could see a little bead of mud that had seeped in. In the gaps between rocks, thicker flops of mud had formed. They reminded me of the new mortar oozing between the stones behind the henhouse.

"Do you think the door will hold?" she asked.

"I don't know." With my finger, I wiped a bead of mud away from the bottom edge, then kept my eyes on the cleaned stripe of wood. "There's no water coming in behind it. At least we don't have to worry about drowning in here."

Barbie crawled to my shelves and dumped the coffee cans, clawing around in the contents. "Don't you have anything here to dig with?"

"There's no use," I said. "This cave is solid rock."

"Well, we have to try, at least. Do you have any better ideas before we suffocate?" She went to the door and dragged a coffee can across the top like a shovel. The scraping was maddening. I could hardly stand how crazy I felt. This was no way to die.

I put on Odum's cracked glasses, plugged my ears with my fingers, and lay back on the mattress of blankets to stare up at the swirling ceiling. All the times I had lain here, reading comics or just going away inside my head, and I never imagined what was really surrounding me. I looked for shapes in the colors, like looking for shapes in the clouds, and I saw a dragon lying on a bed of jewels.

And then I was the dragon. A powerful wizard had taken me prisoner, locked me and my treasure deep inside my own mountain with a magic spell. Because the jewels held secret powers only I knew how to use. They could bring any object to life—or kill any living thing. The wizard wanted this power to rule the world.

Suddenly the dragon felt the mattress of jewels tremble

beneath him. Shaken by the princess, who had this very afternoon been cast into the dragon's lair because she wouldn't marry the wizard. She had been weeping for hours. Her body trembled with grief and fear and shook everything around her.

"Don't cry, dear princess," the dragon said. "I won't eat you."

"Princess?" she said. "Did you just call me princess?"

The dragon's magical jewels suddenly disappeared. In their place were walls of nubby gray rock flickering with candlelight. The sight of the bulging plywood wall brought me back to the Hole in the Wall. And there sat Barbie, twisted around to look down at me, her face tear-stained, Odum's cracked glasses dangling from her dirty fingers.

"Have you finished digging us out yet?" I asked.

"I'm a queen, thank you," she said. "And all the magical spectacles in the kingdom belong to me."

I grabbed them back. "Well, I'm the dragon, and what's yours is mine. But I'll let you borrow your *spectacles* if you rub my back."

"The last time I rubbed your back, a natural disaster happened."

"Oh, come on. Do you want me to die itching, or with a smile on my face."

"I guess I can dig at your crusty old scales. Give me the spectacles, dragon."

I handed them to her, rolled over onto my stomach, and closed my eyes to fly away inside my head. The dragon sang the secret words that gave the jewels their power, and the entire mountain came to life. With a rumbling noise, the rock walls pulled away, forming a tunnel like a giant throat. The queen packed the jewels away into the dragon's pouches, then climbed onto his back. We flew out of the mountain's mouth on our way to a new world. And then the treacherous queen had to go and ruin it. She started pulling the dragon's armor off. Which was my T-shirt.

"Hey, what are you doing, Queen Shish?"

"Didn't you notice that you're not stiff anymore? The colors flew away. Or I thought they did." She held a candle close to my skin. It felt warm. "Some kind of shadow is still there, like a faint bruise. But with the glasses on I don't see the colors swirling anymore. I think they left."

I sat up and wriggled my shoulders around. Then I pulled my sweatshirt over my head. She was right. I could move normally. My back wasn't stiff anymore. "I'm better! All better!" I almost grinned my head off, then slumped, remembering. "Just in time to die. I wish I could see Jed one more time. And Ma. And Grum. And . . ."

"Pa," Barbie said.

"Yeah, him too."

My heart started beating hard, and I felt the hot pressure of tears welling. I hated crying in front of Barbie, but there was no place to go. What a blubbering mess I was. Making myself sick. My stomach churned and all of a sudden I gagged. Up came Sunday dinner. Except why did it smell sweet?

"Oh, wow," said Barbie, staring down at my mess through the glasses. "You've done it again, Seb."

I grabbed the glasses and saw skinny twirls of color spinning up out of little black dots in the roast and potatoes.

"Are those raisins?" Barbie said, plugging her nose as the colors faded and the truth hit.

"If they are, they've been in my stomach since Thursday," I said with a sinking feeling. "Oh, man, my snacks! That *stuff* must have gotten into them, too. No wonder I've been feeling so crappy lately."

Barbie leaned over the bits of pretzel that the chickens had jumped away from and studied them. "Yep," she said, handing me the glasses. "They've got it, all right."

The pretzels flickered with blinky colors like the rocks. "Strange—why don't the colors just fly out of the pretzels?" I wondered. "How did the stuff even get into the pretzels, if this cave has the power to draw it out of me and the chickens? I just don't get it."

"Me neither. And you know what? We never will!" Barbie howled and ran to jump kick the plywood. Then she collapsed in a heap and started to cry again.

"C'mon, Shish." I pulled her over onto the mattress beside me. We curled up together like we must have inside our mother long ago and cried ourselves to sleep as the candles burned low.

I doubted we'd ever wake up.

∽ 17 ∾

It was the darkest of dark nights and a weight pressed down on my stomach. Celery was still my chicken twin! The cookie dough was still in my guts! I was living a nightmare! Then the weight lifted with the sound of wings fluttering and a squawk, and I remembered we'd saved the chickens at the Hole in the Wall. I smiled to myself in the dark, until I remembered the rest of the afternoon and felt my heart go into double time.

The candles had gone out. Had they run out of air to burn? Or just melted down? I groped around for them and couldn't find anything but cold rings of wax. I did feel kind of dizzy, though, and the air was hard to breathe. Barbie slept next to me, taking shallow breaths, and I could hear the restless chickens moving around.

Ma's chickens. Ma. We'd probably never be found. After a couple of days searching, she'd think we had run away like Jed. She'd spend the rest of her life thinking we didn't want to live with her anymore. She didn't deserve that.

I did run away once. When I was eight. I climbed onto the roof of the henhouse and stayed there all day, waiting for someone to notice I was gone and come looking for me. Finally I got too hungry to wait any longer and went inside. Everyone was gathered around the TV watching a sit-com. I stood in front of it jumping up and down to block their view.

"What's for supper? I'm starved. Didn't anyone miss me? For Pete's sake, I ran away this morning," I hollered.

"Did not. You were here for lunch," Barbie said.

"You make a better door than a window," Jed said.

"Did I hear someone say 'for Pete's sake'?" Grum shouted from the bathroom. "The Lord knows . . ."

"Oh, there you are, Seb," said Ma. "Did you have a good time on the roof? We ate all the goulash. Make yourself a peanut butter and jelly."

"You know better than that, Claire," Pa said. "Young man, get your sorry *blankety-blank* to bed without supper. That'll teach you to miss a meal when it's on the table."

Nobody had even worried about me. I guess they'd already gotten used to me going off by myself. In fact, at this very moment, even though I'd been gone for hours and hours after she told me not to go anywhere, Ma probably wasn't really worried about me. Mad, yes. Worried, no, not yet. She was probably sitting in front of the TV with her Word Search. Maybe sipping a glass of wine, since Pa wasn't there. She never drank with him. Joking with Grum about how I'd be grounded for two life sentences when I got home. Make that three life sentences for dragging precious Barbie into my life of crime.

I didn't want to spend my last minutes thinking about bad stuff. Barbie was sleeping so I took the magic glasses off her and let my imagination go wild as Sebastian Alfred Daniels, Space Explorer, finding new galaxies and discovering new kinds of natural resources for our dying planet, and sweet things to munch on, until Barbie woke up.

At first I thought she was having one of her nightmares, with all that screaming and kicking her way out of the covers. But she was wide awake. She grabbed me and hyperventilated, "Sebby, is the plywood caving in? Is this the end?"

And then I heard a noise humming outside like insects in your ears. A sound I knew well from all the time I'd spent in the gore. "Barbie, someone's out there! Someone's coming with a bulldozer!"

Breathing got really hard. I could hear Barbie wheezing. No, that was me wheezing. But someone was coming for us! We held each other and didn't talk, just worked at breathing. I thought about all the new things I would do, and all the old things I wouldn't do anymore, if only we could wake up alive in our own beds tomorrow. And then the engines stopped. What did that mean? Were they going away?

Oh, no! Maybe it wasn't a rescue. Maybe the bulldozer had just come to tear up the oasis, finally mine every last ounce out of the gore's rocks! I had no sense for how much time had passed. Maybe we'd slept through the night. Maybe it was Monday morning, a regular workday at ORC.

I leaped up and pounded on the door and screamed, "Help! Help! We're in here!" I pounded like the door was someone I'd wanted to punch for a long time, pounded and pounded and screamed and screamed until I don't think it was even real words coming out of me. I didn't have the magic glasses on. And it was pitch-black, but I was seeing all sorts of bright colors all the same. I was in a rage. Man, I wasn't ready to die. Not anymore. Not with actual people nearby.

And then I couldn't scream anymore because my lungs had no air. I felt so dizzy, my legs melted out from under me as if they'd lost their bones. I was going to die five minutes before we were found. Typical me. It actually struck me as kind of funny. I started giggling between drags for breath. And crying. All at once.

Barbie knelt next to me and held my face and said, "Sebby, hold on! You can do it."

And then another noise started, the most beautiful music in the whole world. It was the *scrape scrape scrape* of shovels in dirt.

Now Barbie jumped up to pound on the door and scream for help. Only not the wild and crazy way I did. And the scraping noise got closer. And finally the top of the plywood inched away. A strip of midnight blue sky appeared. Moonlight and voices poured through the crack—a man, a woman, hollering our names.

"Ma!" Barbie screamed.

"You kids in there?" The outline of a familiar left hand appeared, pulling at the edge of the plywood. I never thought I'd be happy to see that hairy fist.

"Pa!" Barb squealed. I just moved my lips because I didn't have the energy to speak.

Then a mannequin-smooth right hand joined the hairy left one to yank on the plywood, and the face that appeared sideways in the open space all nose and grin didn't belong to Pa. It was Boots Odum, saying, "Thank God we found you in time. Back away, kids, so we can get some good swipes through this mess with the dozer."

Barbie helped me crawl back to the narrow end of the cave and we huddled together with the chickens, hugging and laughing and crying. The plywood groaned as the bulldozer pushed away the dirt behind it. Finally the darkness ripped away, and the world opened up in a sudden burst of headlights. Soon the familiar shape of Ma filled the doorway, outlined by the brightness like an angel. There should have been trumpets.

"Barbie! Seb!"

"Ma!" I pulled in a deep breath of the cool earthy air that she seemed to carry in her open arms.

She fell to her knees and pulled me and Barbie together into a hug and laughed and cried until she shoved us away. "How dare you two scare me like that? You didn't come home for supper, so I went looking for you, and found all sorts of strange things out in Jed's castle and the henhouse. Scared me half to death! I followed your bike tracks into the gore, and—are those my *chickens*?"

From outside the cave came an urgent voice: "Ma, rescue now, talk later!"

Jed! I could hardly believe my ears. And then he appeared in the blinding glow of the headlights, using a shovel like a walking stick. Only it didn't look like our old Jed. This Jed made a taller and thinner silhouette than the brother who had left home. And he lumbered along in a slow, jerky movement as if the legs he walked on weren't his own. As he got closer, I saw that his legs were wrapped up in some sort of braces.

"Jed!" Barbie cried, and ran out of the cave to throw her arms around him. Then she pulled back and looked him up and down. "What happened to you?"

Stanley Odum stuck his head in. "Hurry on out of there, now—we still have a long night ahead before we can be sure you kids are safe."

Those words scared me and got me wheezing again.

"Oh, I'm so glad we got here in time!" Ma pulled us back into another hug that practically broke my back. My normal, not itching and not stiff anymore back. Then she picked me up on my feet and started walking with me, but my legs were limp and I fell back down. Like the world's strongest weight-lifter she curled me right up in her arms and carried me to Odum's pickup truck. Barbie came along behind with Jed. We all loaded into the back and then Boots Odum jumped into the driver's seat and took off. The bulldozer whined along behind with a goon in the cab. We soon outdistanced it.

It felt so good to be alive, with Jed among us, looking up at the almost full moon and all the stars winking. I didn't even wonder where we were going as Ma explained that she'd followed the tracks to the gore and called Stanley Odum for help. To her surprise, Jed was with him when he showed up at the house.

And now Ma asked the questions we all wanted to know. “So, Jed, do tell us—where have you been all this time? Why wouldn’t you talk to us when you called? Why did you even leave us?”

“I was at . . .” Jed hesitated.

Now that my eyes had adjusted to the moonlight, I realized just how different he looked now, not just his body but his face. He looked a lot older than eighteen. His eyes were sunken and sad. He had a new scar on his right cheek, all the way from his eye back to his ear and down to the chin. He had a scraggly beard with thin spots that I thought might be covering scars, too.

“I was at ORC.”

And of course we were all bursting with questions about that until Jed gave us a warning look and gestured toward our driver.

“Folks, I really can’t tell you a lot of it. Well, I could tell you—” He grinned his old grin and he didn’t look so aged and beaten down. “—but I’d have to kill you.”

That was one of Jed’s favorite jokes, but at the moment it seemed more scary than funny. He cleared his throat and said, “Sorry. But honestly, a lot of it is top secret. Classified stuff. I wasn’t even supposed to be calling you at all, and I didn’t want my calls traced. I had to sneak around.”

Ma had me cradled in her lap, and the pickup bounced along on the rib road like a baby buggy. Man, I hadn’t felt this spoiled since I carried a blankie. She reached over to stroke Jed’s arm sympathetically. “How much can you tell us, honey? What happened?” She ran her finger gently down the scar on his face. He turned his head away and stared off toward the mudslide.

"I was snooping around in places I didn't belong. Like some other people I know—" He paused to squint at me and Barbie. "And one day I had an accident. A terrible accident. A long fall. Broke my head open. Broke both legs while I was snowballing down. Landed in a crater of nasty water. Somehow dragged myself halfway onto land, even though I don't remember doing it. I was almost dead when one of the ORC guards found me. I didn't wake up for a week."

"You didn't run away on purpose?" Barbie whispered.

He drew a deep breath and pressed his lips together tightly, shaking his head. "And I'm sorry you had to think that, believe me, but it was better than the alternative." Then he continued his story. "At first I thought I was in a hospital. My legs were all bandaged in casts held up in the air with pulleys. Traction, it's called. My legs had been broken and twisted and—it's hard to explain. They looked like pretzels before the surgery. Stan showed me the pictures."

I knew what he'd left out. My back had been there. "Your legs were petrified," I said.

He licked his lips nervously, craned his head to look through the cab window at Boots Odum, then shrugged and nodded. "Sort of. Petrification is the replacement of organic material with minerals, through capillary action, and it takes hundreds or thousands of years or even longer. What happened to me is called adrification. I was the first human it happened to . . . well, at least to this extent. They didn't know what to do. They performed surgery to straighten my legs out, but I'm still not normal. The adrium is still in my tissues."

"So that's what it's called," said Barbie. "Adrium."

We all knew he was talking about the substance that ORC was mining from the rocks.

Jed nodded. "Based on the Hindi word for rock. A new

element that Stan discovered. So far, it hasn't been located anywhere else on earth. It has unusual properties of attraction, but it's, well, I can't go into it very far. Besides having to kill you if I tell you, it involves a lot of science that I don't completely understand yet myself. But suffice it to say, from what we know so far, some isotopes are stable, some are unstable, some are right-handed and behave one way, some are left-handed and behave another way, and the more we experiment—"

"Wait!" I blurted. "Adrium has hands?"

Jed smiled crookedly in the moonlight. "Handedness isn't just about hands—it's about which side is dominant. And the harder we try to figure it out, the more trouble we get into."

"You say *we* a lot," Ma said. "Are you working for ORC now?"

"Not yet, but someday maybe. Obviously I've had a lot of free time, and Stan's been teaching me some things. You'll be happy to know I've finished my high school diploma already. As soon as we find a cure, I'm going to start working on degrees in biochemical engineering and physics. But I can't go to college with these legs." He gave his left brace a slap.

"You seem to get around all right," Ma said.

"True. The problem is we don't know yet exactly how the adrium poison spreads, and we don't have an antidote yet. Until we know it's contained, Stan says we can't risk exposing the public."

Did he say *poison*? "Thanks a lot for nothing!" I said, punching his arm. "Are we going to be prisoners at ORC now like you?"

"Seb, I'm not a prisoner. I'm in secret quarantine. And you, dough boy, have already been exposed. Everyone at home may have been. Our property has the most intense concentration of unstable adrium I've—whoops." He looked over his shoulder again. "Forget I said that."

The pickup had bumped to a sudden stop. Stan Odum was showing his hairy hand to the electric eye that opened the security gate. After all those spying missions, I was finally entering the Onion.

18

Now that the truck had stopped, I heard Barbie's teeth chattering. Mine decided to join hers. We'd gotten chilled in the cave, and riding in the open air had sucked any remaining warmth out. On the bright side, I noticed that my teeth didn't ache anymore, even when they clanked together like ice.

Jed put an arm around each of us and rubbed our shoulders briskly as he said, "Don't worry, guys. Stan will take good care of you. He's really a good fella underneath all the bulldozers. The Gash to the Onion was graveled with good intentions."

Boots Odum a good fella? This was not the same Jed who used to picket outside the entrance to ORC, protesting the ruin of the land in the gore.

The truck spiraled downward through a parking garage with several floors. The top floor held all the huge equipment under the height of the dome—bulldozers, dump trucks, backhoes. The middle floors held more cars than I'd expect during the wee hours of Sunday night. There must be more people working here than I ever realized.

On the bottom floor, we passed a bunch more vehicles—one, a very familiar rusty red pickup. Me and Barbie gaped at each other.

Ma seemed stunned. "What's your father's truck doing here?"

We all looked at Jed.

"I'll explain later," he whispered. "The walls in this place have ears. And eyes. Beware."

We went all the way to the end of the spiral and stopped right next to the entrance on the bottom floor. We must have been pretty deep underground. The parking spot had the number one painted on the concrete and a RESERVED CEO sign posted on the wall.

"We're here." Jed scooched himself to the back of the truck and lowered the tailgate, then dropped to the floor, moving better than I expected him to in his leg braces. "Come on." He held out his hand to help Ma down.

"Alrighty, then," said Boots Odum, joining us. He hoisted up his jeans by the belt loops, reminding me so much of Pa that I stepped behind Ma. "I realize you folks will want to know why I brought you here instead of taking you home. Unfortunately, there's a lot I can't say. Some questions simply don't have answers. Some things, I can't say because of classified information. So please bear with me."

"Classified by whom?" said Ma in a tight voice, her arms crossed over her chest. "Are you working for the government, Stan?"

Boots Odum ignored that and continued with his welcome speech. "One thing I do know is that we have to scan you all immediately, just to make sure you're all right."

"All right," said Ma, her arms still crossed. "Why wouldn't we be all right?"

He winced at her apologetically, then looked at his watch. "We'd better hurry."

I wanted to ask why the rush, but I figured that was classified too.

Our host stepped to the entrance, showed his hand to another electric eye, and led the way past a series of wide elevators down a long hallway with white concrete block walls, like at school. I followed at his heels, taking it all in.

The legendary boots clickety-clacked on the hard tile floor and left a faint trail of leathery aroma along with clods of mud they were tracking in. Jed's steps went THUMP unevenly behind us, like one leg took longer than the other, but he kept up.

The walls had lots of doors. Some had normal department names like Human Resources or Payroll, and some had mysterious names like Project Foobar or Little Genius Lab. Every door had a security scanner. You probably had to let an electric eye scan your hand to use the bathroom if you worked at ORC.

Occasionally an archway would curve off into another hallway, reminding me of the passages in the tunnel where we'd found the cavern. A strange sweet scent that I recognized right away drifted from one hallway.

"I know that smell from somewhere," said Ma.

"What is that smell, Mr. Odum?" I had a pretty good idea it was adrium, but I wanted to hear what Boots would say. He didn't answer, so I stopped and turned on my heels at the arch with the sweet smell. "Where does this hallway go?"

"Believe me, you don't want to go there, brother," said Jed, grabbing me by the shirt neck and hauling me back in line without missing a step.

Finally the boots stopped at a double-wide door. With another hand scan, it slid open, and our host bowed with his right arm gesturing grandly, "After you, ladies and germs."

Jed took my hand firmly as we entered. The lights weren't as bright and harsh here, and blue carpet softened the floor. The first thing I noticed was a pot of daffodils in the center of a large wooden table with fancy upholstered chairs around it like somebody's dining room. To our right was a nurses' station with nobody behind it. On the far side of the daffodil table, pastel striped curtains dangled from steel runners in the ceiling. Some curtains were pulled across to make rooms like in the hospital where we had visited Grum when she broke her wrists. Other curtains were tied back, showing empty beds.

"My old room," Jed said, pointing to a bed with steel posts that rose up at the four corners supporting a box-shaped frame overhead. From the steel frame dangled all sorts of pulleys and ropes and a metal triangle like a super-sized coat hanger.

A woman pulling a white medical jacket on over green hospital clothes came yawning out of a doorway behind the nurses' station. Her light brown hair was bedraggled, and her cheek had a deep sleep crease. As the door slowly closed behind her, I noticed a tousled bed. Maybe she lived here all the time, like Jed. How many other people did ORC have tucked away living secret lives?

"Good evening, Dr. Mills. Sorry for the short notice," said Boots Odum. The woman wiped her eyes and yawned, "S'all right." After the yawn finished, she said, carefully pronouncing every sound, "I am here to serve, Mr. Odum."

"Thank you nevertheless, doctor," he said. "How is our newest patient?"

Dr. Mills frowned and glanced toward the closed curtains. "Life signs are stable for now."

Boots Odum nodded. I felt Jed's hand fall lower. His shoulders had slumped. What had deflated him?

"Hello, Jed," said the doctor with a big smile in her voice. Water sounds splashed behind the tall counter as she washed her hands. "Good to see you looking spry."

"Thanks, doc." Jed tipped his head to her. "Wouldn't be here without you." He turned to Ma. "Dr. Mills is the one who saved my life and fixed my pretzels so I could walk on them."

The doctor and Boots Odum exchanged worried glances. "Pretzels!" He chuckled, giving Jed a fond pat on the shoulder. "Your colorful expressions always entertain me, son, but you don't want to give your family the wrong idea, do you? Pretzels." He chuckled some more.

"He doesn't want Jed to give us the *right* idea," Barbie whispered in my ear.

The doctor looked me up and down as she came around the counter, snapping purple gloves onto her hands. "You say the boy is already infected?"

Boots Odum quit chuckling and nodded. "Ingested. And I want the girl scanned, too. Then Mrs. Daniels."

The boy. The girl. You'd think he'd figure out our names if he was going to kidnap and scan us and maybe make us disappear from the face of the earth like Jed did for all those months he was being held in *secret quarantine*.

"My name is Barbara," the Shish said. "You can call me Barb. Only my family is allowed to call me Barbie. And this is Sebastian. Everyone calls him Sebby."

"Say cheese," I said, waving toward the ceiling where a video camera pointed straight at us. Then it moved on in a slow circle, capturing the whole room.

"Pleased to meet you both," said the doctor, seeming to mean it. She looked really nice when she smiled even though she'd looked like a plain grumpy person when she'd walked out of her sleeping room. "And Mrs. Daniels." She reached out to shake Ma's hand. Ma reluctantly brushed fingers with her.

"Sit down, Claire, and make yourself comfortable," Boots Odum said with a nod toward the daffodils. "I'll get the paperwork for you to sign and see if I can rustle us up a cup of coffee while we wait."

Ma didn't sit, though. She stepped between Barbie and me and pulled us close. "Where they go, I go." I squeezed her arm to thank her. She squeezed back.

That dahlia bulb nose turned bright red. Obviously Boots Odum didn't like being contradicted. His lips pressed tight and he said, "The scanning room is designed for the patient and the doctor. Dr. Mills is not going to hurt your kids."

"There won't be any scanning of these precious bodies until you tell us why," said Ma, locking Barbie and me under her arms. "I'm not letting you do some top secret classified experiment on my kids without knowing what it is! You're about two inches away from a lawsuit, Boots."

Hoo, boy, he didn't like being called that. He stiffened like an adrified chicken with its mouth open, unable to cluck.

Just then a jazz riff played in his shirt pocket. He took the phone out and glanced at it before rolling his eyes and tossing his head impatiently. "Look, I'm trying to help you, Claire. I have a lot to do right now, and you're not making it any easier." He flipped the ringing phone open as he lifted it to his ear and said irritably, "Yes, what is it?" He stepped away and turned his back to us, carrying on his conversation in hushed tones.

"It's fine, Ma," Jed said gently, touching her arm. "Really. We're just checking to make sure there isn't any—anything seriously wrong. It's like an X-ray or an MRI. It won't hurt the twins. Believe me, I've been scanned plenty of times. Saved my life." He crossed his heart.

Boots Odum turned briskly and said, "Doctor, we have a situation developing in Section A. I must trust you to take things from here." And with not so much as a glance at us, he scanned his hand and took off running down the hall, heels clickety-clacking an urgent beat.

My stomach flipped when I saw that someone's hand needed to pass a test to get *out* an ORC door, not just *in*. I closed my eyes and prayed we'd be allowed to leave. Never thought I'd be so homesick for the musty air of our teeny tiny house. And Grum. She'd tell these people what's up and what's down.

Dr. Mills's eyelids fluttered rapidly as she watched the door slide closed, and a vein in her neck pulsed. She put her hand there in a way that made me think of Miss Beverly. "Mrs. Daniels, may I have your permission to scan Barb and Sebby now?"

Ma nodded numbly. Jed sat her down, and the doctor handed her a clipboard with papers to fill out.

"Barbara, please wait here until I'm finished with your brother. Sebastian, please follow me."

We crossed the infirmary and entered a wide door. The doctor sat at a desk with a control panel and computer monitor over it, built into a wall made of green tinted glass.

"Before you go into the scanner, Sebby, I need to ask you a few questions," she said, pulling up a roller stool for me to sit on. She wanted to know all the diseases I'd ever had (none, except colds, chicken pox, and growing pains) and all the bones I'd ever broken (none, except Barbie's arm once by accident when I jumped on her). Then she asked about everything I'd had to eat or drink for the past few days, how many times I'd gone to the bathroom, and what everything looked like when it came out.

"Do you want to know about—?" I gave her the universal barf signal.

"Oh, yes," she said. "Tell me about your nausea."

I made it as descriptive as possible, kind of hoping to gross her out, but she kept a straight face the whole time. Since I didn't know how much to trust her, being ORC's secret quarantine doctor and all, I did leave out a few details. Such as, how the barf raisins looked through the magic glasses. Which I didn't tell her about borrowing from her boss. Or, where I happened to be when the cookie dough came up. Because I didn't think it was any of her business that we had an amazing secret tunnel on our property. And I didn't talk about my adventures with Celery since I didn't eat or drink her. In fact I wasn't planning to eat chicken or eggs ever again.

"Now please remove your clothing," the doctor said.

I was afraid of that! "All right, but don't look."

She smiled a little and turned her back. When I said I was ready, Dr. Mills pressed a button. With a ringing sound, the glass wall opened wide. "Step inside, please."

The scanner's insides looked like a fancy shower with lots of doodads and gadgets on the walls and ceiling. "Cool!" I pressed my nose against the glass and made faces.

"Very attractive," said Dr. Mills. "Now stand in the middle and hold still, please." I heard her like she was talking in my ear.

I did as she asked, and Dr. Mills started the machinery. It sounded kind of like a band playing slow music. Beams of all different colors came at me from every direction, something like the disco ball that sends light bouncing all over the Skate Away, except this light was warm. With my eyes closed I pretended I was at the seashore. Surfing. Uh-oh, wipeout! Dragged in the undercurrent. Up for air just in the nick of time. What happened to the beach? It's gone—nothing in sight but water water everywhere. And sharks! *Aaaahhhh!*

"Sebastian, could you please hold still," said a voice.

Whoops, there went my brain making stuff up. I should

have pretended I was a rock at the beach. "Sorry, doc," I said, and smiled apologetically.

"Oh, my! Could you open your mouth wider, Sebastian? A little more? Yes, and tip your head back. A little to the right. Yes, that's perfect—hold, please." The scanning machine clicked and whirred and played some more dance music as colors came beaming out of the light jets into my mouth. It made my eyes cross trying to watch until the doctor asked me a question.

"Sebby, have you been to the dentist recently?"

"No, but interesting you should ask. My teeth have been killing me. I didn't tell you before because my grandmother said it wasn't a mysterious debilitating illness. She said I was getting my twelve-year molars."

"Indeed, you have those *and* your wisdom teeth."

"What? I can't have my wisdom teeth yet. I'm still a dumb kid." I knew a little about wisdom teeth because Jed had just gotten his first one shortly before he disappeared.

"Oh, you're not dumb," the doctor said. She kept asking me to pose this way, then that way. It seemed to take forever before she finally said, "Okay, finished," and the door slid open.

As I jumped into my clothes I asked, "Doc, what were you looking for? What's wrong with me? Besides wisdom? It's my bones, isn't it. I've grown, like, six inches since Thursday."

"That is an unusual growth spurt, isn't it," she said.

"Does it have anything to do with the raw cookie dough I shouldn't have eaten?" I asked. She didn't respond. "I'd really like to know, doc. They're my bones."

"I'm sorry, Sebby, but I'm not at liberty to discuss the situation with you at this time."

She escorted me to the seating area and invited Barbie in for a scan. Ma jumped up. "Wait, Dr. Mills—aren't you going to tell me if my son is all right?"

Hey, yeah! Maybe the doctor would be at liberty to discuss my situation with the Higher Power of Ma.

With her hand on the door, the doctor turned to Ma. "Please be patient for a while longer, Mrs. Daniels, while I complete the scans of your daughter and yourself. Mr. Odum will discuss the results with you after we have had a chance to analyze the data."

"Stan will discuss it with me? You're the doctor, aren't you?"

Dr. Mills smiled. "Try not to worry, Mrs. Daniels." Then she made eye contact with Jed and flashed him a quick smile. That must have meant something to him, because he took Ma's hand and whispered, "It's okay, Ma, Sebby will be all right."

All right, maybe, but completely wiped out from the colored-light attack and posing. I flopped down onto the row of chairs next to Ma and put my head on her lap. As she ran her fingers through my curls I fell into a sound sleep. When I woke up, her lap had slipped out from under me, and Barbie stood over me with her hand across my mouth.

I sat up, rubbed my eyes, and looked around. Jed stood behind the counter where the doctor had washed her hands. The lights went out, and he said, "Whoops, sorry," before they came back on. Something in the ceiling beeped. The video camera stopped still, its lens turned upward.

"Hurry, follow me," Jed whispered urgently. He crossed the room and pulled aside a set of closed curtains. My chin dropped at what I saw: a wall of cages holding animals like in a pet store. A horned owl sat still as a statue, except it slowly moved its head to follow the motions we made. A Doberman on the bottom row sat frozen like a statue except its skinny tail, which it wagged like crazy when it saw us. All of the animals had wires and tubes hooked up to them, and monitors flashing numbers behind their cages.

"Isn't that one of Ma's chickens?" Barbie said, pointing to what looked like one of Celery's aunties.

We both looked accusingly at Jed. The bald spots in his beard reddened. "I'll explain all that later. No time now. C'mon, it's the next bed."

Jed closed that curtain and hurried to yank the next curtain aside. And this time I froze with the shock. A cold feeling drained down my neck all the way to my feet.

"Pa!"

He was in a hospital bed tipped like a teeter-totter with his head up, his arms still out to the sides like a cheerleader, and his feet poking the sheet at the same angle we'd first spotted his shoes that night outside Jed's castle. The only thing that moved was his eyes. They flitted around rapidly when he saw us, but it was impossible to tell what he was thinking.

"It's a *hard* life, isn't it Pa," said Jed.

"What happened to him?" I didn't laugh at Jed's joke that time. My lower lip wouldn't stop quivering. I took a few small steps toward Pa, my hand out.

"Pa's suffering from adrium poisoning, just like in my legs." Jed spoke very fast, in a hushed voice. "The adrium has spread through his entire body. He's almost completely paralyzed."

"How did he get here?" Barbie asked. Exactly what I wanted to know.

"Long story," Jed said. "Tell you later."

"He's like the chickens," I said. "What happened to him? And them? And you?"

Jed peeked out around the curtain before answering in a whisper. "Stan hasn't figured it out yet, but I have, and I'm not telling him or he won't be able to resist getting his hands on our property. He has connections—and if Ma won't sell out willingly, he'll get the courts to force her. Seb, Barbie, we have to work together. I'll tell you what I know, but you two need to use your brains and be careful what you say. Can you do that?"

He was shaking me by the shoulder now.

"Jeez! I know how to keep my mouth shut." I bit my lips shut to prove it.

"All right. See, there are microscopic particles of adrium left in the waste slag after extraction from the ores. Those particles want to get back to an adrium vein. It's like a magnetic force, and very, very powerful. What Stan doesn't realize is that we have the mother lode on our land. A pure adrium vein. All that leachate water from the gore fights its way onto our property because it's attracted there. Pa got poisoned because he spent the night passed out in a leachate puddle in the yard."

Huh? I didn't get much of that, but Barbie nodded as he spoke, like she'd already figured it all out too. She said, "And the chickens also soaked up that leachate stuff when they went into their hidey-hole, right?"

"Right. There's a lot more to it, but we don't have time to dawdle. Quick, Seb—how did you get rid of that contaminated dough you ate?"

But I was still trying to figure out his explanation. "What's the adrium got to do with Ma and Pa getting into a fight? Do you know how much money Boots offered to buy—"

Barbie reached out and pinched my lips shut. "It happened in the tunnel behind our henhouse. Sebby heaved up the dough in the big cavern near the wall where you left us the warning letter. He had a petrified, I mean *adrified,* chicken stuck to him—long story—and the chicken was cured too. All the *stuff,* the *adrium,* just flew right out into the walls. That cavern looks like living jewelry when you wear the magic glasses."

"I get it! Back to the mother lode . . ." Jed huffed out all his air and rolled his eyes back, looking up at the ceiling. "Oh, crap. Why'd I have to go seal that barrier up so tight? It's going to take half the night to rip it down. By then Pa could be dead."

꩜ 19 ꩜

"Dead?" me and Barbie echoed. The owl hooted on the other side of the curtain. Eerie!

Jed nodded grimly. "When only part of the body is affected, you can usually live with it. Like me. And Stan—he lived half his life with an adrified hand."

"So that's why he has amazing bionic fingers!"

"It's not something he advertises on his billboards, but, yes, Seb. Anyway, different animals have different levels of tolerance. Birds are tough. That owl's been here longer than I have. Humans aren't tough. Last week there was a . . . well, an industrial accident. Three guys got soaked. All dead in twenty-four hours. Pa's not going to make it much longer without some sort of miracle cure."

"But—how can ORC get away with that?" I said. "Three guys dead? There wasn't anything on the news. Grum would have been gabbing our ears off about something like that."

Jed checked outside the curtain again. He was getting really nervous, I could tell by the twitching around his eyes. In a low voice I could barely hear, he said, "Look, half the people who work here never go anywhere. Nobody even knows they're here. It's as if they don't exist."

Barbie was pacing in arcs around Pa's bed, biting off her beloved fingernails. "Jed, I know you don't want Boots Odum to find out about our adrium vein, but this is a matter of life and death! We should tell him about how Sebby lost his dough so he can help us save Pa! And all those poor animals . . ."

"No way!" I waved my hands across her face. "We can tell him how I lost my raisins instead. On his property."

She hit her hand on her head, looking a lot like me for once. Except for the hair. "I knew that," she said. "That's a way better idea." She patted my arm admiringly, for the first time ever. My face got warm and probably had a silly smile on it.

Jed looked as confused as his explanation had made me. "Raisins . . . huh? What's this idea?"

"There's another place where the miracle cure happens," I told him. "The Hole in the Wall, where you rescued us tonight. That's why we went there in the first place, to save Ma's chickens."

"The paint flew out of Sebby's back there, too," Barbie added excitedly.

"Paint out of Sebby's back . . . ? Oh, never mind. Tell me later. There's no time to waste. We're not waiting for Stan." And Jed started yanking Pa's cords and tubes out of the wall. This was a job I could get into. I leaped to his aid.

"What about Ma?" Barbie said, looking out the curtain toward the scanning room door. "We can't leave without her."

Jed said, "Yes, we can. When Ma comes out here, so will Dr. Mills, and Dr. Mills works for Stan. She is not going to let us take Pa out of here without security clearance. There's no time for that. If we want to save Pa, we're going to have to leave Ma to take care of herself. Let's go!"

"I'm not leaving Ma." Barbie crossed her arms.

"Suit yourself," Jed said, and gestured for me to help him roll Pa's bed.

We were almost at the door when a buzzer started ringing

from somewhere that sounded like everywhere. A red light blinked overhead, and a voice came over the intercom, "Security Protocol Aegis Shield in effect. Repeat, Security Protocol Aegis Shield." Man, oh man, was I scared.

The door to the scanning room flew open, and Dr. Mills ran out with Ma close behind, looking confused. They practically fell into Pa's lap.

"Craig!" cried Ma in a voice that no words could describe. She looked like the shock would have exploded her head if she wasn't holding her face together with her hands.

"Busted," I said, thinking this would be the end of life as I knew it. No more homework, no more church, no more of Ma's hockey puckburgers—we were all going to disappear in the guts of ORC forever and ever. But Dr. Mills surprised me.

"Oh, thank goodness you're here to help, Jed. Get your father and the rest of your family out, and I'll take care of Miss Beverly. Go straight to the Boys of Summer Stadium, and report to Zone Q."

"Miss Beverly?" me and Barbie both said as Dr. Mills threw open a door next to her own room. Sure enough, the long-necked Miss Beverly was sitting up in bed looking confused.

Jed called, "I'm on top of it, doc," and flashed me and Barbie a crooked grin as he held his hand out to Ma. "Come with us, Ma."

"Hey, shouldn't someone rescue the Dogstars, too?" I asked, feeling pretty proud of myself for figuring it out. "They must be somewhere behind a curtain back here. Right?"

"Huh?" said Jed. "Who?"

"The hippies at Zensyl—"

"Hurry!" cried Dr. Mills.

At that, our family skating skills came in handy as we raced Pa's roller bed up the long hallway, dodging the people who were popping out of doorways and archways. Everyone ran as if their lives depended on it. It was dizzy-making chaos, the scariest two minutes of my life. Which was saying a lot, considering the minutes I'd been having lately. I had to hold on hard to my corner of the bed and run along with the tide of people mostly in pajamas as the buzzers and lights blared and the loudspeaker kept repeating the same message over and over, Security Protocol Aegis Shield, Security Protocol Aegis Shield. That meant to evacuate immediately, Jed shouted when Ma asked. It felt like one of those movies where everyone has to jettison out in the pods before the spaceship self-destructs.

The elevators and the door to the parking ramp were bottlenecked with people waiting to get out with suitcases on wheels, files on hand trucks, and carts loaded with equipment. Someone had jammed a nutty candy bar under the door to keep it propped open, and the security alarm was going crazy. My stomach growled. I eyed the candy bar and started to bend over for it, but Jed yanked me back to attention.

As soon as we squeezed through, Jed called, "To Pa's truck!"

We pushed the bed up the ramp, veering around cars and trucks squealing out of their spots. It seemed that the compound went on for acres, maybe even a mile, underneath the ground. The place was like an iceberg, and the Onion top was only the tip of it.

After an eternity we got to the truck and loaded Pa into the back, leaving the hospital bed in the next empty space. Nobody even made any jokes about how ridiculous he looked in his hospital johnny, like we would have if we weren't all in a terrified panic. Ma climbed in back with me and Pa while Barbie jumped into the front with Jed. He fished the keys out of his pocket, honked the horn, and butted out into the line of traffic. He kept honking and scooting around other cars that were backing out, forcing the truck's way up and out of the Onion.

At the exit a security goon waved traffic along toward town, but instead Jed veered toward our side of the gore. "This isn't the way to the stadium!" Ma cried. "The doctor told us to meet her at Zone Q! What does your brother think he's doing?"

"Saving Pa's life," I said, holding on tight to the side of the truck. We were bumping along Odum's Gash like bobsled racers. Jed leaned intently over the steering wheel. Driving couldn't have been easy for him with his stiff leg braces. Every few seconds he checked the rearview mirror. I kept looking all around, watching for goons, but nobody was following us.

"Seb, it's time you told me what's been going on," Ma said sternly. And so I told her. Just about everything. Well, maybe not everything. But enough to satisfy her, while not getting me grounded in the next life. Until the truck bounced to a stop at the Hole in the Wall.

The oasis looked different now. So much for the bright, moonlit sky. Clouds had covered our world again. The dark outlines of living trees stuck out of the mudslide. No longer did the trees dangle upside down from the cliff above. They had slid down to the ground and been buried, mostly, with a few roots sticking out here and there like creepy zombie hands in a cemetery.

Jed left the headlights shining into the cave and hopped out to open the tailgate. "We have to hurry. If the adrium containment shield blows, it'll take the whole gore with it."

We each took an arm or a leg, all four of us—Ma, Barbie, Jed, me—and carried Pa inside. Talk about heavy as a rock! Jed said Pa probably wasn't much heavier than normal, though. "He just feels that way because he's deadweight."

"Ooh, deadweight," said Ma. "I think that adrium stuff twisted your sense of humor."

"I take offense at that, Ma," said Jed. "My sense of humor has always been twisted."

The chickens clucked and gathered around, expecting hand-outs of grain, but all they got was Pa plunked down with a THUD. "Here you go, ladies," I said, rubbing my hands and making Ma laugh nervously as she adjusted Pa's johnny to cover his sprawled legs.

"I still can't believe what you told me on the way over here, Seb," she said. "Colors flying out of chickens into rock walls. It sounds like some fantasy out of a children's book!"

"How long does this take, anyway?" Jed said, looking warily down at Pa.

"The chickens only took a few minutes," I said. "Do you feel anything?"

Jed looked down at his legs and smirked. "You know, I didn't even think of that!"

"You could see if anything's happening if you had the magic glasses on," Barbie said.

"Dang!" I said, feeling my pockets. "I lost them."

"They must still be here somewhere," Barbie said. Both of us got on our knees and felt around in the blankets where we had gone to sleep just a few hours ago.

"So that's where Grum's quilt went," said Ma.

"Aha, here we go." I found the glasses and handed them to Ma.

She put them on and made the predictable noises. "Incredible. The stone is alive." Then she stared intently at Pa. I couldn't tell whether she was hoping he'd come back to life, or hoping he wouldn't. I wasn't sure what I thought about that myself. And then I felt bad for not being sure. You shouldn't want your father to die, should you? But I couldn't help but think it would solve a lot of problems. Then he wouldn't have to decide to stay or go, to change or not change. We wouldn't have to be scared of his temper anymore.

"Do you see any colors swirling out of him, Ma?" Barbie asked. Ma shook her head no and handed Jed the glasses. He gaped all around at the cave walls and tipped his head back to examine the ceiling. "Wow, this place is gorgeous. No wonder Stan couldn't bear to mine his childhood getaway."

"Huh?" I said. "What do you mean, *his* childhood getaway?! I mean, I know he owns the property, technically, but . . . but . . . ," I sputtered. Everyone was giving me strange looks.

"Seb, this cave belonged to Stan before you were even a glint in Pa's eye," Jed said. "If not for this cave, Grum would probably still be living in the gore and Stan Odum would probably be a starving artist next door. He used to hang out here as a kid. The walls would sometimes seem to blink colors at him, and he became a scientist just to figure out the cause. That's why he started ORC. He believes that the power of adrium could fuel distant space travel, if it can be controlled. There are exciting possibilities for adrium as a clean source of energy. At the very least it would have many uses in industry, medicine, defense, you name it. Anyway, this was Stan's secret place first."

"Oh," I said.

Jed started pacing around, jostling elbows with everyone in the small area of the cave. He hit his head on the ceiling and rubbed it. "Shoot! Shouldn't something have happened to Pa now?"

"He's not a chicken," I said.

"That's for sure," Jed said. "He'll fight with anyone."

But for once I wasn't joking. "That's not what I mean!

The adrium flew out of the chickens quickly, but it didn't leave my back right away. I don't really even know when it happened."

"Sometime after I scratched your back," Barbie said. "Remember how itchy it was?"

Jed nodded along with me. "Itching is one of the early symptoms of adrification. My legs itched so much when I first woke up, I used to reach down my casts with chopsticks to scratch. When Dr. Mills caught me, she took away my chopsticks and gave me a turkey baster to squirt air instead. After the casts came off she gave me heating pads. That really made the stiffness and pain feel better."

"Hey, Shish, it's been a long night. How about another back rub?" I said, throwing myself stomach down on the blankets. She kicked me instead.

"Back rub? You mean you didn't just scratch—you massaged?" Jed asked.

Barbie nodded. "For quite a while."

Jed grinned with realization. "Heat! Of course!" he said. "Adrification cools the body. Massaging gets the blood circulating, warms up the body, and must help release the adrium. Well, what are you all waiting for? Let's get to work warming up the old man. We're going to have to get out of here pretty soon before the Onion blows."

We all stared down at Pa: his face stuck in a stupor, his fingers in a choke hold on his imaginary pom-poms, his hairy shins cocked off to the sides of his johnny gown. Then we looked at each other and sort of grimaced and giggled, all nervous and feeling ridiculous. Nobody wanted to touch him, until Ma dropped to Pa's side and started to massage his thighs with a vengeance.

"Craig, honey, come back to us!"

I had an idea. "No, no, do his legs last. That way he can't chase us when he comes to."

Us kids started laughing then! We even got the chickens cackling. "Brilliant!" said Jed.

But Ma yelled at us. "You kids stop that joking around. He's your father and he's in serious trouble." But she did move her massaging up to Pa's arms.

"Wouldn't it be awesome if Pa woke up on his good side?" Jed said in a dreamy voice.

Could that really happen? The thought of it took my breath away. At that moment the thing I wanted most in the world was for Pa to wake up and be his old self. In case he could hear, I said, "Sorry I was an idiot, Pa," and got down on my knees to massage his face. Barbie worked on his chest, and we propped him onto his side so Jed could get behind him to do his back.

After a few minutes Pa's icy skin warmed and softened into something like clay. His muscles started to twitch. Ma and Jed traded the glasses back and forth to watch the adrium colors fly to the walls. A little later, Pa slowly reached his right hand up to his chin. I jumped all the way out of the cave, in case he was reaching for me, but he just wiggled his jaw around.

The first hoarse word that came out of his crooked mouth was a *blankety-blank*. Then, "What the *blankety-blank*'s going on! Where the *blankety-blank* am I! Why do I feel so *blankety-blanking* stiff! And what the *blankety-blank* am I wearing!" He pulled on the chest pocket of his johnny gown. Then he jerked around like a newborn fawn trying to get up, but he couldn't. We must not have been massaging his good side.

We all looked at each other, waiting for someone else to answer.

Ma adjusted his johnny again. "What's the last thing you remember, Craig?" she said.

Pa glared at her. "Why do you want to know?" He acted like he had something to hide. Not good. I took another step away. My eyes prickled, but I scowled back the tears.

Finally Pa managed to move his arms and torso enough to lean on his elbows and turn his head slowly, taking in the cave. It reminded me of that owl back in the infirmary. I hoped Dr. Mills had gotten those poor animals out along with Miss Beverly.

"This looks like that old cave where Stan and I used to hide from our old ladies when we were brats," Pa bellowed. He pounded the ground with his fist. "Why did you bring me here? What did you do to me, Claire? When I—"

Just then his neck stopped turning. His eyes got big. They had stopped on Jed. Pa really did look like an owl, and not the sweet kind perched on a branch but an owl with its wings spread wide, swooping down on a baby skunk it was ready to devour. "You!" he roared. "You're behind this, aren't you? Why, I'll—"

The top of his body twisted and his arms lashed out, but he couldn't get up because his legs were still paralyzed.

Ma had been calling his name over and over, trying to get Pa's attention, but all he had owl eyes for was Jed. She took a fistful of Pa's hair and turned his head toward her. "Craig, whether you know it or not, you owe your life, such as it is, to your kids. They rescued you. And nobody got you into this sorry shape but yourself, Mr. Do-Drop-Inn. Rumor has it that there's going to be an explosion under your butt tonight. So if you want to walk out of here alive, I suggest you get to work rubbing the stiffness out of your legs."

And she walked very calmly out without looking back. Pa kept screaming and yelling behind us as we all scurried to follow her lead. I felt like a duckling following my mother.

But suddenly she turned around and very calmly retraced her steps, saying, “Oops! Forgot the chickens. Just ignore the howling lunatic while we gather them up. He’s made his own bed.”

Well, that was like saying, “Just ignore the pizza until you finish your math.” I looked straight at Pa. His desperate eyes locked onto mine as he bellowed, “*Blankety-blank,* son, *help* me! Please!” And like old Celery the adrified chicken, I was magnetized. I walked toward him, my hands held out.

“That’s my boy,” he said. “Just let me pull myself up with my arms across your shoulders, and you can drag me home.”

But that wasn’t good enough. “No, Pa. We have to finish massaging your legs now so you can walk.” And I got down to work below the knees. I leaned over to concentrate on what I was doing so I wouldn’t have to see his face. He looked . . . not like himself. He was humbled and ashamed.

“Sebby? What are you doing?” Ma crawled from behind the shelves with a struggling hen. “Oh . . .”

When she saw what was going on, she melted like mozzarella. She knelt at Pa’s feet to join the massage, saying, “Don’t you dare make me sorry I did this, Craig Daniels.”

“Oh . . . kay,” he whispered, then swallowed hard and looked at the wall. I knew what he was doing, though, because I was trying not to do the same thing. But a couple of hot tears dripped onto his legs anyway. I rubbed them in fast.

Jed and Barbie each claimed a thigh. We’d been at it for a couple of minutes when the whole gore started to tremble. We felt it in the floor, and we felt it in Pa.

20

"We have to get out of here *now,*" Jed cried. "Pa, can you walk?"

Pa grunted and flexed his ankle. His toes wiggled. His thigh muscles twitched. Sweat popped out over his eyebrows. "I can't bend my knees," he said. "You're gonna hafta help me."

We got him to the truck. Ma took the keys from Jed. "You kids ride in the back," she said in her "no buts" voice. We all knew she wanted to talk to Pa alone. Which was fine by me. I didn't know what to say to him now anyway. It was all so weird.

"As soon as we get home," said Jed as the truck took off, "you two have to help me take down the plywood I nailed up to block our tunnel. Pa and I have to get to that adrium vein—"

"No, Jed!" said Barbie. "Wait until after the explosion. What if the tunnels collapse when you're back there?"

The two of them kept talking, but I couldn't concentrate on words. The ground alongside the rib road was actually heaving all around. I felt seasick, bouncing around in the truck bed. Ma had the pedal to the metal, and we were practically flying over the bumps. Even so, I was terrified that we wouldn't get out of the gore in time. We still hadn't even left the rib road, and we had a long stretch of the Gash still to go. On and on we lurched, and then I heard that noise. That same wind-chime ringing musical noise that had filled my head when I flopped the pebble around in the sunlight, when it wobbled away in the cavern—and when I got too close to the egg painting in Boots Odum's workshop. Oh, man, if I was hearing that again, something big was about to happen.

"Do you hear something?" I said, grabbing Barbie's arm.

"It's the adrium," Jed said, not sounding pleased. "It makes that sound when it moves."

"When it moves?" That freaked me out. The sound was getting louder.

"Well, when certain isotopes of certain chirality—oh, never mind. I don't really understand it myself. Stan calls it the music of the spheres. But anyway, nothing good ever comes after you hear it, I can tell you that."

As if I wasn't scared enough already. We prayed for our lives until the truck finally reached the back gate not far from our house. For the first time since ORC had built it, the gate stood wide open, with no goons standing guard over it and no vehicles in the employee parking spots. Ma didn't even let off the gas but barreled on through to Kettle Road.

We left the gore and entered a different world. All four wheels of the truck gripped ground at once. The road felt solid, while behind us the gore heaved faster and faster. We watched it in the blinks between the giant rocks that bordered Kettle Road.

Ma jolted the truck to a stop in our driveway. As she opened her door she called, "You kids help your father into the SUV. We're switching vehicles and getting out of Dodge as soon as I fetch your grandmother."

I jumped over the side of the truck. "I'll help you, Ma." I ran ahead of her to kick the door in, but it just hurt my foot without budging. Like the cave door after the mudslide. But on the bright side, this time it didn't hurt my teeth.

"She must have bolted the door," Ma said and knocked hard. "Mum! It's Claire! Come quick—it's an emergency!"

When the door groaned open, Grum stood leaning on Pa's rifle. "I sure am glad it's you," she said. "A couple of Stanley Odum's *employees* came by here an hour ago and tried to *evacuate* me, but with the help of my special walking stick I persuaded them otherwise."

"Well, I hope you'll come with us now," Ma said, "because the Onion's gonna explode and it could take our property with it."

Grum nodded. "Of course, we're all ready." She turned around and pointed to a stack of garbage bags in the living room.

Ma looked both amused and astounded. "What did you pack?"

"Everything we'll need to live for the first month if we survive the holocaust," she said.

With half a smile Ma shook her head and said, "Let's pray we won't need all that. But good idea just in case. Sebby, you hurry up and load the supplies while I help your grandmother into the car."

Man, some of those bags were heavy. She must have packed every can of Spam and cast-iron skillet in the place. From the porch I hollered, "Barbie, Jed, come help—"

Pa was in the back of the SUV, but Barbie and Jed were nowhere to be seen. They must have gone out to the henhouse to take down the plywood. Jed was going to follow through with his plan! He'd go out to the mother lode and be there when the gore exploded. Then who knew what disaster would happen next! I couldn't let him go there. I couldn't lose my brother again.

“Jed!” I screamed, throwing the Spam bag into the trunk on my way to the henhouse.

I bounced smack into him as he came out backward. I ricocheted onto my butt in a puddle. Great, now I was soaking wet with that leachate stuff! “Aaaaahhhh!” I jumped up and batted at my soggy pants.

Then I felt something move around my ankles. I looked down. The puddle had started to vibrate, and the water swirled in curlicues toward the road. I stared in disbelief.

“Seb, don’t just stand there, help me with this tent,” called Jed, stuck in the henhouse door.

“Do you see this water?”

“Yes, which is why we need to hurry up and get out of here.”

“Seb, hurry up and load these supplies!” called Ma. She had Grum halfway to the SUV.

“You heard your mother,” Pa called out the window.

“Ahh!” I cried, covering both ears.

“I’ll help Jed with the tent,” Barbie said from behind him. She was carrying the camp stove.

My mind flashed back to our last camping trip at Lake Exton, and how much we’d bickered over who would carry what, and how happy we were tipping Pa out of the boat when he took us fishing. But this was not a happy moment at all. I shook the memory loose and ran to load the bags, hurdling the streams of curlicue water along the way.

Soon we had the SUV packed to the roof and barely any room left for us kids to sit. Ma couldn’t even see out the back window to drive.

Just then Jed’s Stupid Cat came running out of nowhere, leaping over all the rivulets to jump up on Jed’s legs and lick his hand.

"There's no room for the cat." Pa scowled, but he sounded almost sad.

"What do you say we take two cars," said Jed. "I'll drive Fluffy Kitty and the kids in the truck."

"Good idea," said Ma, handing him the keys. "Which way are we going?"

"Left," said Grum quickly from the passenger seat. "Just get on the interstate and drive."

"I vote for that. Get as many miles between us and that *blankety-blank* gore as possible." (That was Pa.)

"Let's decide on a place to meet," said Jed. "In case we get separated."

"How about that campground we used to go to on Lake Exton?" suggested Ma. "Assuming Boots doesn't blow up the whole county. If that happens, where we meet is a moot point."

"Granted," said Jed. "See you at the lake. Or in the next life."

"Pray for good weather!" Grum hollered out the passenger window as the SUV took off down the driveway.

Me and Barbie climbed into the truck. The cat sat on Jed's lap with his head out the window. Jed adjusted the seat from where Ma had left it, turned with a grin, and gave us the ol' Daniels eyebrow.

"Uh-oh," said Barbie. "Why do I think I'm not gonna like this?"

"You two ready to see a show?" said Jed.

I grinned and browed him back. "You didn't say *when* we'd meet them at the lake."

Jed waited until the SUV had driven out of sight. Then he turned right toward Kettle Ridge. He parked at the top facing the gore like a giant drive-in movie screen. Which it kind of was, for us, since we were watching everything on the edge of our seats and wanting to know what would happen next.

From here the heaving ground looked almost alive, as if a giant insect lay underneath and was trying to break free from its cocoon. The ORC Onion, which wasn't normally visible at night, glowed with swirling colors and shadows. A line of vehicles slowly moved along the Gash toward town, their headlights like strings of polka dots.

While we waited for something else to happen, Jed stroked Stupid's head until the cat flopped over onto his back and offered his belly. "Good boy," Jed said. "I sure missed you all these months, Dawg."

"You mean he wasn't with you?" Barbie asked in surprise. "He disappeared when you did, and just showed up again Thursday."

Jed had petted away a good size hairball by now. He flicked it out the window. It drifted and caught on the windshield wiper, looking just like the hairballs caught on the chair legs in Miss Beverly's kitchen. It made me wonder. "Jed, was your cat at the Odum's?"

He looked impressed. "How'd you figure that out, Sherlock?"

I explained about the chair legs. "Plus there was a picture of him on Odum's screen saver in his workshop. Hey, that really was your handwriting in the poodle joke, wasn't it!"

He grinned. "Stan likes my handwriting," he said. "I've seen that image you're talking about. It's called Arnold's Cat Map and it has something to do with one of Stan's theories about how adrium works. But it's not Fluffy Kitty in the picture—it just looks a lot like him."

"Wait, back up, how did your cat wind up at the Odum's?" Barbie wanted to know.

"When the goons found me, Fluffy Kitty was sitting on my

chest and meowing. He followed them all the way to the Onion. Stan took him home to keep him safe inside the house and to keep Miss Beverly company. But he got out one day last week, and he must have found his way home. Good thing he didn't get into the adrium."

"He somehow knows to avoid that stuff," I said.

"Jed's Smart Cat," said Barbie with a smile.

"Oh, yeah, something else I've been wanting to ask you. How did you know about the dough in my stomach?"

"Miss Beverly tells Stan everything. Usually at least twice."

Duh! Of course. Miss Beverly was the only one outside the family who knew about it. If I'd thought of that combined with the other clues in the workshop, I might have figured out that there was some connection between Jed and Boots Odum.

Just then sirens started wailing in town, blending ominously with the music of the spheres. "Whoa," I said. "That doesn't sound good."

"Jed, are you sure we're safe here?" Barbie asked.

"Can't say I am. But if the explosion takes out this whole solid ridge, then we wouldn't have been any better off going in the other direction, either. Let's find out what's going on."

At that he reached into the side pocket of his cargo pants and pulled out something that looked like a cell phone. He flipped it open and pressed a button. I leaned over his arm to look. It was a miniature computer, with a screen lighting up on one side and a digital keyboard on the other. After a moment the screen filled with tiny symbols streaming along.

"What the heck? How can you read that?"

Jed put something over his eyes that looked like swim goggles with green lenses. He grinned like Boots Odum.

"Yikes! You look like an insect," said Barbie.

"No, a space alien," I said. Those lenses fit perfectly over Jed's eyes. They were the exact same size and shape.

"Cool! Can I see?"

Jed handed me the goggles. Excitedly I pulled the strap around my head, but the lenses only covered the outside corners of my eyes. "I can't see anything. What the heck?" They were just green. Like a blank chalkboard.

Jed took the goggles back and put them on. "Custom made for my eyes only. Stan invented the technology. Calls it the Little Genius System. Top secret stuff. Don't tell him I showed you, or he'll have to kill me."

He turned his face toward the computer again. The symbols on the keyboard blinked rapidly, as if invisible fingers were typing a hundred words a minute, and then suddenly the text disappeared, replaced by images of landforms—North America, the U.S., and then a big dark triangle shape sunk deep into the rolling hills, with something round blinking in the middle like a dim mood lamp.

"The gore!" I said.

Barbie leaned over me leaning over Jed and grabbed the computer to see. Then she looked out over the actual gore and said, "Amazing."

There were still a few vehicles emerging from the Onion, heavy equipment mostly, looking like Tonka toys. Jed moved the satellite image over toward town, and we saw a traffic jam of vehicles from Main Street Kokadjo packing the highway toward Exton. All the vehicles were headed that way, even in the breakdown lanes, except for one of ORC's security Hummers. That was stuck in front of Skate Away trying to get through the opposite way, heading to the edge of town.

A little way past the traffic jam, at the bottom of Kettle

Ridge, a huge dump truck from the strip mine had been parked to block the road. After that the pavement made an empty black ribbon until the very top, where one lonely red pickup sat overlooking the gore. Jed zoomed the image in on Stupid. I mean Fluffly Kitty. He had jumped out the window and was now sitting on the hood like a gargoyle.

"Cool!" I said. "Hey, can we look at the commune?" Maybe we'd find some clue about why the Dogstars left Zensylvania in Odum's hands so suddenly.

"Not now," he said. "There's something else I need to check out first." And he whizzed the image straight over to the Boys of Summer Stadium. Its parking lots were full, but the field and the stands were empty.

"That's weird," said Barbie. "Where did all the people go?"

"Where do you think?" said Jed, as if it should be obvious.

"To buy hot dogs?" I said.

"That's outrageous," said Barbie.

"Then they must have beamed up into the government's secret starship."

Jed laughed and tousled my hair. "I missed you even more than Fluffy Kitty, bro. No, everyone's gone to the bomb shelters underground."

"Oh," me and Barbie both said. Hers was the *oh, of course* kind and mine was *oh, is that all.* Sometimes the truth is pretty boring.

"Didn't you ever wonder why a little podunk town like Kokadjo got a stadium? Sure, people come from all over the county for the games and concerts, but the real reason Stan had the stadium built was to have an emergency evacuation site for ORC. Adrium is too volatile to handle without major precautions. And all his computer servers are backed up at an underground lab there. All his technology, all his research. The walls are so thick, everyone and everything down there could survive any disaster."

"Then why didn't we go there like everyone else?" squealed Barbie, punching Jed's arm.

"Because when this is all over, sis, everyone else there will be able to go home and live happily ever after. But not us. The whole Daniels family will be stuck in Zone Q until Stan says we can leave."

"Q for quarantine!" I said.

"You got it, bro. And I've had enough of it. I'm betting that Stan knows adrium doesn't spread from person to person. What he doesn't want to spread is the truth about what's going on at ORC. Most of the people who work there don't even know."

Jed's computer keyboard blinked some more, and the symbols came flooding back onto the screen, too tiny for me to see.

"Yep, that's what I was afraid of," Jed said.

"What?!" I said.

"Those goons stuck in traffic down on Main Street? Stan sent them after us. He's not too pleased that we didn't show up."

"He's not the only one," Barbie said, pointing.

A car was squealing wheels around the corner of the kettle, headlights on high. An overloaded SUV, to be exact.

Ma pulled up beside us and jumped out. The SUV kept shaking, though. The good ol' jackhammer was sound asleep among the garbage bags. Grum stayed in the passenger seat, jawing her dentures. We hopped out of the truck.

Ma hugged us and then started hollering at us. "Thank goodness you're safe! But I've had enough of you kids giving me the slip. You could have told me where you wanted to go, you know. Instead you . . . and then . . . all the streets are one way, and that's O-U-T, out! Do you realize how difficult it was to convince the police to let me past the road blockade? I told them—oh dear God! Heaven help us!"

She'd finally caught sight of the glowing Onion below. She paused to gape.

The music of the spheres had grown louder, the perfume smell stronger. The air prickled with some kind of energy. Or maybe it was just my nerves.

Then that old song "The Devil Went Down to Georgia" started blasting from Jed's leg. He pulled out his pocket computer. I ran over to see. The screen was lit up and all of a sudden we were looking inside some kind of office filled with computer screens and consoles with gizmos, and the backs of about ten heads.

"Sorry, guys. You aren't supposed to see this," Jed said, turning his back to us. Me and Barbie kept a polite distance, but I wriggled my head under his arm so I could look at the computer screen.

"Hey, Stan," Jed said. "You rang?"

Suddenly the image changed to all face, mostly dahlia bulb. Red. "Jed! Where the fantod are you, son? I need you here pronto!"

Jed put his hand over my face and pushed me out of sight. But I could still hear.

"Sorry, my friend, no can do," Jed said. "It's my day off. I'm spending some quality time with the family."

"Look, you know I can't leave you out there running loose. This is an evacuation. You know the risks. You know where you need to be."

"I know where you want me," Jed said, "but my family has to come first. I'm sure you can understand that."

"Of course I can. That's why you have to get them to the stadium, ASAP, for their own good."

"Oh, really?"

"You know the containment field has been breached. This is the only place I can guarantee their safety, son."

"And after the dust has settled, you'll let us go home?"

Boots Odum didn't answer right away.

"That's what I thought. Don't worry, we can take care of ourselves, Stan. I'll let you get back to work now. We'll catch up another time. Peace out."

"Jed! Wait! Please. Listen to me. That little brother of yours had enough adrium in his system to cause accelerated bone growth, and yet there's not a trace of the element remaining in his body. He's been cured somehow! He must be studied!"

Woo-hoo! I was cured! I looked up at the starless sky and punched a *Yes!* to the Big Guy.

"Look, Jed, I don't have time to dillydally. You want to continue putting yourself and your father at risk, fine. But you aren't the only ones who need that cure."

"Is that really all you want from us, Stan? To find the cure?"

Odum paused before saying in a high voice, "Of course!"

I didn't believe him. If I'd thought about it, I might not have done what I did next. But I am who I am, so I grabbed Jed's computer and told Boot's Odum's nose, "Liar! You want to steal our land!"

"Seb!" Jed put his hand over my mouth with one hand and took back the computer with the other. "Sorry about that, Stan. He's a little impulsive." He turned his head away from the computer and winked at me before continuing.

"If all you want is the cure, Stan, then I'll be glad to tell you. But first you have to promise you'll leave us alone."

"What? Son, you know I can't in good conscience leave you alone! There has to be a controlled research study. I'll have to examine you folks after this is all over. For heaven's sake, tell me what you know. My mother is—"

But his sentence got cut off by Ma snatching the phone. "Stan, Jed is not your son. You don't get to tell him what to do. And you know very well what he means. No more of your secret quarantine business. We'll be happy to help you with your precious research, but we'll come and go as we please. And we won't be selling our land to you, either. Unless of course your little unnatural disaster tonight destroys it. In which case I'll send you the bill."

Just then the siren from town grew louder. The Hummer must have made it through the traffic. It was blaring its way up Kettle Ridge!

Jed grabbed the phone back. "Oh, one more thing, Stan—call off your men. Now! We're not going anywhere with them. Deal or no deal?"

"All right, all right!" Odum cried. "I don't have time to waste! Deal! What's the cure?"

"Just go to an adrium vein like the one where we found the twins tonight, apply heat to the adrified area, and the infection will be drawn from the body. Like mag—"

The computer screen went blank. Suddenly the sky filled with flashes of color. Sounds struck the air like an orchestra during the grand finale. I felt vibrations in my bones. We all looked out over the gore with fear and awe.

21

Grum appeared at my side and gripped my arm so hard, I thought it might drop right off like a pruned branch. Over her own glasses she had propped the cracked magic glasses. Ma must have given them to her.

"Dear God, it's the second coming," she said. "Everybody repent your sins and get right with the Lord while you still have a chance!"

"You may be right," said Ma, getting a couple of lawn chairs out of the trunk for her and Grum. They sat, leaned their heads together, and started praying.

I stopped listening. Words didn't mean anything. I was so awed. The most vivid bursts of every color I'd ever seen were flying up into the sky from all around the Onion. You didn't even need magic glasses to see them. Colors whirling around in circles, then swooping down into the ground. The air smelled so sweet, I almost couldn't bear to breathe. The music sounded like all the noises of the woods and the ocean—yet, just wind.

The mined gore dirt started throbbing with those same swirling patterns we'd seen on the cuckoo wall and my tattoo, spreading out and out from where the colors landed, all the way to the fence of boulders that bordered the gore. It seemed that the colors were rushing along like water in rapids, whirling and spinning down into the earth. Down and down. The loose soil was actually sinking deep and hardening into swirls. I sure wished I could tell what was happening at the Hole in the Wall, but it was impossible to see. I felt sad about losing that place.

"Cowabunga," a deep voice said behind us. It made me jump out of my sadness.

"Dude," said another.

I turned to stare up at two of the biggest guys I'd ever seen who weren't on TV wrestling. Odum's goons had arrived. They looked more like twins than me and Barbie. Both wore gray uniforms and phone earpieces, and they both had on the pearly magic glasses. Those guys looked even more amazed than the rest of us, which gave me an idea.

"Excuse me, Sir, can I borrow your glasses for a second?"

"Sebastian!" said Grum, shaking my elbow. "Say *may* I."

"May I?"

Goon One and Goon Two shrugged at each other. "The Chief said be nice to these folks," Goon One said, and Goon Two replied, "What can it hurt? Let the kids have some fun." So they handed their glasses over to me and Barbie, then turned around to talk to the voices inside their ears.

The magic glasses made the colors in the gore even more intense, like in the adrium mother lode. They also showed me something I hadn't noticed before, a swirl of colors flying up toward Kettle Ridge like a swarm of butterflies. It was pretty incredible. I watched the adrium swarm approach until suddenly Jed let out a yelp and fell onto his back. He rolled over and clawed at the weeds that dotted the roadside, yet somehow he was sliding backward, toward the gore, his fingers scraping the ground.

"Heeellllp!" he howled.

And then I realized what was happening: the adrium inside his legs was dragging him! Like Celery and the rock had flown me! I leaned down to grab Jed's hands and pulled as hard as I could. Ma's arms went around my waist and she pulled on me. But the adrium was too strong for us. Jed's hands slipped free, and I tumbled to the ground with Ma.

When I hopped back to my feet and wiped the dirt out of my eyes, Jed was belly up to the guardrail, his legs beneath it poking into the gore, with Barbie holding him by his belt. I was terrified he'd get yanked in. Why weren't those big goons trying to help, for Pete's sake? They were still turned around talking on their ear phones, that's why, with their fingers in their free ears to block out all the noise.

I ran at them flailing and screaming to get their attention. When they turned and saw what was happening to Jed, they immediately lunged to the rescue. They each took an arm, dug in their heels, and held him back.

Then I leaned over the edge for a closer look at Jed's predicament. He was so terrified, his mouth was frozen open without any scream coming out. But his legs were—amazing! Sticking straight out into the air, with colors swirling all around them! The adrium in his legs was leaving to join the swarm.

Pretty soon Jed's screaming transformed into a goofy grin. His knees flopped and he dangled his legs over the edge, kicking his feet like he was sitting on a dock splashing in the water.

"Thanks, fellas, I think you can let go now."

"No problem," the goons said, and stepped back. Grum applauded. "Well done, boys." Barbie and Ma clapped, too. I wolf whistled.

Jed pulled his legs out from under the guardrail and leaned his back against it with a deep breath. Then he grinned down at his braces. Slowly he unbuckled them and set them aside. Then he crisscrossed his legs and slowly wobbled to his feet.

Ma ran to put her arm around him. “Let’s get you away from that edge, huh?”

He took a step forward and his legs folded under him. So he was back on the ground, but still goofy grinning.

Ma smiled, too. “My baby’s learning to walk.”

I reached out to give Jed a hand. “C’mon, you big baby.” Barbie took his other hand. We yanked him up again, and this time he stood firm.

He took one step, then another. We let him go.

“How do you feel?” Ma asked.

“*So* glad I didn’t let Stan give me bionic legs,” Jed said through his grin. He just couldn’t stop grinning. He walked all the way to the SUV and sat on the bumper, rubbing his thighs. The SUV was still vibrating with Pa’s snores.

Pa!

How could he have slept through all this? After all he’d been through, he must be exhausted. But I couldn’t let him snooze away this chance to be cured like Jed! I ran to the door and slid it open.

Pa fell straight out onto the ground in a backward somersault, as if he’d been leaning hard against the door. “What the . . . ” He yelled all the usual cusses. But I didn’t care what he called me. I just cared that a bunch of colors came butterflying out along with him. It was like they’d been waiting at the door. They circled away and disappeared over the edge of the cliff.

Pa’s eyes just about filled his face, he looked so surprised. He stopped hollering and hopped to his feet with a big smile. He did a squat and then a lunge and then started lifting me by the waist to put me on his shoulders, like he used to when I was little. Except I was almost as tall as him now, and he couldn’t lift me.

My father groaned and grimaced and put me down. Then he put his hand on the small of his back and croaked, "I'm fine, fine. Don't worry, I'm fine. Where we gonna pitch the tent?"

Finally he looked around and realized where we were. "Oh."

By now the music of the spheres had quieted, and the color explosion had faded. The sweet smell had lifted, leaving behind the scent of mud after a spring rain. Everything seemed almost normal.

Pa shrugged and said, "Wake me up when we get there." He climbed back in among the garbage bags.

"Is the disaster over?" Ma asked the goons. Obviously they knew everything there was to know through their technologically advanced ears.

"Close enough for horseshoes," said Goon One. "You folks are authorized to go home. We've been assigned to escort you and assure the safety of the premises before you enter."

Ma harrumphed.

"Claire, do you want to get me my *special walking stick*?" said Grum.

That would be pretty amusing, I thought, Grum pulling a gun on the goons. But Ma put her hand on Grum's shoulder and said, "That's all right, Mum, I think Stan is good for his word, if nothing else." Then she turned back toward the goons. "Gentlemen, I appreciate it, but we won't be requiring any escorts or assurances. You're authorized to leave us alone. Kids, give these gentlemen back their glasses and say thanks."

Dang. I was hoping! I dug the glasses out of their hiding place in my pocket and held them out to Goon One. "Thanks."

"No problem."

"Just one more thing," he said, turning to Jed. "I'm going to have to confiscate your Little Genius." He held out his hand.

Ma's face crinkled. "His *what*?"

"He must mean me," I said, even though I knew he didn't. "Odum wants me bad."

That joke got me a groan from Barbie. Jed was groaning, too, but not for the same reason. "No! Really? Stan gave me that system for Christmas! He can't take it back!"

"Sorry, kid. Company policy. Security clearance required. Yours has been revoked."

"Unless, of course, you wish to return with us to the stadium," said Goon Two.

Muttering like Pa, Jed felt around in his pockets, then pulled out the green alien bug-eye goggles. He dangled them and shook his head sadly. "What a waste of resources. I'm the only one who can even use this unit."

"Nevertheless," said Goon One, stepping closer. I wondered if I ought to fetch Grum her special walking stick after all. But Jed gave in. He muttered some more and dropped the goggles into the big meaty outstretched hand. The men thanked him and got into the Hummer.

"Why didn't they make you fork over the computer?" Barbie asked. I was wondering the same thing.

"Without the headware, that's just a fairly intelligent cell phone. If Stan wants it back, he can call me."

Smiling at that, we loaded into our vehicles to leave. "This time, I'll follow you," Ma said to Jed.

He had just turned the ignition when headlights cropped the ridge. A shiny black pickup truck was coming our way. "That's Stan!" Jed smacked the steering wheel. "I can't believe he's coming for us after he made a deal!"

The truck cut us off, goons poured out of it like circus clowns, and we were swept away into the guts of Zone Q forever. In my imagination. Actually, there were only two people in the cab: Boots and Miss Beverly. She gave us a weak smile and a little wave as they sped by. Her son ignored us and careened the vehicle toward the newly installed gate at the Trace.

"They must be going to cure Miss Beverly!" Barbie said.

I smacked my head, realizing. "Zensylvania has adrium! That's why Odum made the Dogstars an offer they couldn't refuse."

"Makes sense," Jed said. "And whatever he paid them, it wasn't enough."

At that, Jed backed the truck out, and we headed for home.

I was pretty nervous about what we'd find at the bottom of the hill. Would all the leachate be gone? Would all our stuff still be there? At least the goons hadn't reclaimed the broken borrowed glasses from Grum. She was wearing them on top of her asbestos curls now. We could use them to scan the property for adrium ourselves.

So much for all our fears and worries. The second I saw the house, I knew things had changed for the better. It actually seemed to stand a little straighter, like Miss Beverly's neck. The front door opened right away as soon as Ma turned the key, no kicking necessary! There was hardly any water left in the basement, and the remaining puddles just looked like ordinary yuck water, no colors except rusty brown.

Same thing in the yard—most of the water had been sucked away, even that almost-pond the henhouse had been swimming in and Pa had soaked in. Plus, there were really cool looking swirls etched into the mud. All the drag marks and footprints had been erased from the night Pa got adrified. The walls in the castle had lost their colors, but there were grayish shadows of swirl shapes left behind there too. I put a cuckoo back on the wall, and it had nothing to say.

When we got done checking everything out, Ma put her hands on her hips, shook her head, and sighed towards the jam-packed SUV. "I'm pooped. Let's hit the hay and leave all that junk to take care of tomorrow."

Just then the car door opened and out stepped Pa, looking fresh as a daisy. "Hey, what are we doing back home? I thought we were going camping!"

"That was when we were running for our lives, Craig," Ma said. "Our property's fine, Stan Odum's off our backs, and I'm going to bed." She turned toward the front steps.

Pa grunted in a sort of disappointed way. He looked at me and then Barbie with a question in his eyes. It reminded me of the look he used to give when he was teaching us something and wanting to know if we'd gotten it—how to start a bonfire, how to worm a fishhook. Then he turned all around, looking for something, someone . . . Jed. Pa's eyes lit up at the sight of him playing chase with Stupid. I mean Fluffy Kitty.

Then Pa stepped toward Ma, calling, "Claire, wait, don't go."

Ma paused at the kitchen door and turned her head toward Pa. Just her head. "What now?"

"We're all packed and ready," he said. "What do you say to a spontaneous camping trip, Mrs. Daniels?"

Cocking her head in amusement, Ma turned our way and looked from face to face. I made prayer hands and begged with my eyes. Say yes, Ma. Say yes!

"Tomorrow's . . . a school day," she said slowly.

"Oh, so what. Let the kids have some fun for a change," said Pa. "We ain't had a vacation in years." He didn't sound all blustery and bossy, though. He sounded a little nervous.

"No school for the rest of the week!" Grum called from inside the house. "They just announced it on the news. All the public water and sewer lines in town have been damaged. Electricity's out all along Main Street too."

"Yay! No school!" I said while Barbie said, "No school? Darn!"

"Well, I guess," said Ma, getting my hopes up, "if you really want to go camping, you all can go ahead and have fun without me. I have to work. We can't afford for me to take time off."

Down went my hopes. What if this Pa wasn't the jolly old camping Pa, just the couch warmer Pa in a rare good mood? I didn't want to go anywhere with him and without Ma.

Pa was still working on her. "You can go to work from the campground, dear. In fact, you'll be closer. It's just a five minute drive from there to the factory."

"That's a fact, but everything's easier at home, getting ready for work, cooking, all that." Ma's voice had a kind of wishful tone behind her excuses, though. We almost had her. I knew she wouldn't appreciate any unsolicited comments from the peanut gallery, so I just begged her harder with my eyes, and jiggled a lot.

"Sebby, do you have to use the bathroom?" Ma asked.

"No, I just really want you to go camping with us."

At that, Pa stepped between me and Barbie and put an arm around each of us. "Myself and the twins'll have the fish all fried up in the pan when you get out of work. Right-o, kids?"

Wow. I nodded my head off, because "Right-o" couldn't get by the lump in my throat. This was beautiful.

"Sure, Pa," said Barbie. She looked pretty pleased, too, in spite of her horrible disappointment at having to go a week without any tests or quizzes.

Ma gave up half a smile, saying, "Well, all right," and then she frowned. "No, we can't. Someone has to take care of the chickens!"

After all we'd gone through to save them, I had to agree, someone did. "How about we get Boots Odum to come clean up their doo-doo?"

Oh, the looks I got! "Just joking," I said. "Just joking." Sheesh. No way did I really want that guy poking around on our property. Especially not in the henhouse with the secret tunnel entrance.

Then Jed stepped into the discussion. Fluffy Kitty had just given up playing with him to chase after a noise in the woods. "Look, you guys can go camping without me. I'll stay here and keep an eye on things. Who knows, there might still be repercussions from the explosion. Somebody ought to stick around, just in case."

"What am I, chopped liver?" Grum called. She was leaning in the doorway now. "Jed, you're going with them, and I'm going to hold down the fort, with the help of God and Smith & Wesson." (That was Pa's kind of rifle.) She had us all smiling when she added, "My mind's made up. Now go." And Grum being Grum, that was the end of that.

Since there hadn't been a holocaust after all, we took out the garbage bags of supplies we didn't need for camping. Then the Daniels family took off for Lake Exton in the SUV, Ma and Pa in the front and us three kids in the back, with Grum standing on the porch waving.

On the way to Lake Exton we listened to the news on the radio. It was all about the evacuation. A representative from ORC came on and said that there had been an earthquake right underneath ORC. This earthquake had led to a colorful explosion of industrial chemicals, but there had been enough advance warning for everyone to get out unharmed. The complex had been completely destroyed, with losses amounting in the hundreds of millions of dollars, but the operations of ORC would continue in other offices. All Kokadjo employees who wished to continue in their jobs would be offered transfers. Upon completion of cleanup, the site would be restored as parklands and donated to the county.

"Wow, that's quite a story," said Ma.

"That lying, cheating, paralyzing *blankety-blanking blank,*" cussed Pa. "He'll be inflicting his shady shenanigans on another innocent town now. Well, good riddance from the perspective of this ol' buddy ol' pal."

"C'mon, now, Pa," said Jed. "Stan never meant to hurt you or anybody else. He's a scientist, after all, and—"

Jed suddenly interrupted himself laughing. It was so strange and unexpected, I couldn't help but laugh too. Then Barbie giggled, and Ma joined in, then Pa cracked up. Ma pulled the car over so we could laugh ourselves out without going off the road. My stomach was sore from it.

"What was so funny, anyway," Barbie said when we were moving again.

Jed smiled sheepishly and said, "Never mind."

But I could guess. I considered it pretty funny myself that the two of them, Pa and Jed, had completely switched sides on the goodness or badness of Boots Odum. But they were still arguing. Some things never change.

It rained most of the time we were camping. We had an okay vacation anyway. We spent long hours in the tent telling stories and playing games. Pa bet Ma he could keep a bonfire going the whole time, and to everyone's surprise, he did. He wasn't the *blankety-blank* Pa anymore. Well, I can't lie—he still swore like a sailor's parrot, but he wasn't a *blankety-blanking blank* himself. He didn't even drink one beer, not even in the fishing boat. But he wasn't the Pa from when I was little, either. Back then he used to spend every minute *doing* something. Now he spent a lot of time just sitting and staring at the lake. I could live with this Pa, though. In fact, I spent some time sitting next to him, until I had a little accident of the imagination and fell in the water.

On the last day us kids gave up waiting for the rain to stop and went out fishing anyway while Pa watched us from the shoreline. It was pretty boring. Barbie had brought a book and umbrella to read under. Jed sat hunched in his rain gear texting on his fairly intelligent cell phone. He'd been spending quite a bit of time doing that and talking to his long lost friends. Even to Boots Odum a couple times.

The two of them had made us all appointments later in the week to go to Zone Q and be examined, but we all got to go home afterward. Jed described to Odum all about how the colors had left his body and Pa's, and how the leachate had left the swirly patterns in our yard, and stuff like that to help ORC study the adrium. But he didn't say a word about the spectacular mother lode on our property. We had a family conference and everyone agreed that was going to stay hidden behind the nailed plywood. We'd never let the land leave the family or allow it to be mined.

"Some things that are found in the ground should stay in the ground," Pa said. For once Jed agreed with him.

So back to the boat. We hadn't caught anything yet, and it was almost time for Ma to get out of work. I really wanted to catch her dinner today. The other days, Pa wound up going to the store for fish so he could keep his promise about frying it up in the pan.

"Here, fishy fishy fishy," I said and cast out the line.

Jed looked up at me. "You guys wanna check your email? Sebby, what's your screen name?"

I shrugged. I didn't get much free time on the computers at school, and I had way better things to do on them than email.

"His would be danielssebastian@stoms.edu," Barbie said, turning her page.

Oh, yeah. I forgot we all had email addresses at school.

"What's your password?" Jed asked.

I shrugged again.

"Try his birthday," Barbie said.

"Eureka," Jed said. "Sebby, you've never checked your email! You have pages of unopened messages from Adele Byron. Isn't that your teacher?"

"Um . . . ," I said. She may have said something about that a few times.

Just then the phone dinged. "New message coming in," said Jed. "From dogstarcluster."

"She lives!" I stuck the fishing pole between my knees and grabbed the phone away from Jed. The Shish jumped up and tried leaning over my shoulder to read the message too. The boat tipped wildly. Barbie teetered all over the place. Pa laughed from the shore.

"Sit down before you fall, Shish, I'll read it to you," I said.

Dear Sebastian,

I hope this message finds you feeling upright and unshaken by the recent earthquake in Kokadjo. As you have probably ascertained by now, my family has left the Love Shack and transferred ownership to the Odum Research Corporation. I regret that I could not inform you about our situation and say good-bye in person.

The good news is, Goldenrod and Marigold have finally discovered that computers are very groovy. Therefore, they have decided to start a new community called Breezy

Acres Ecovillage, where we will operate a wind farm for electricity so we can enjoy technological advances without contributing to global warming through the exploitation of fossil fuels. Currently we are traveling around the country seeking an appropriate location.

Zensylvania would have been ideal, but alas, there is no water there anymore. Our spring ran dry. That is why we moved so suddenly. G & M will not tell me the details of their confidential discussion with Mr. O, but I have a theory. My theory is that the mining in Kokadjo Gore disturbed the aquifer and caused our spring to drain.

GtG! M wants me to help her look for her HS friends on facebook. SIT!

Clstr

It took like ten years to read through the message because Barbie and Jed kept making comments. Well, I did, too. It's always something with Boots Odum. Anyway, at the end of the ten years I was pretty happy to know that Cluster was okay and finally able to have a computer like she wanted.

The next day, something else made me even happier. No, I didn't catch a big fish. On the way home we stopped at the store to buy me red canvas high-tops. And as if that wasn't happiness enough, the sun came out on our way home. So it was shining when we rounded the corner and got our first sight of the new Kokadjo Gore. What had once been beautiful rolling wooded land, and then an ugly hollowed-out strip mine, had now become something else entirely. A little sparkling lake! Reflecting the clear blue sky. Fresh spring water had bubbled up from the earth and filled the deep places. Little gray islands of rock poked up where the slag piles had been.

That night, we sat out in our front yard to watch the bats

swoop down over the rocky shoreline. The lake sparkled like gemstones in the moonlight, making me think of the dragon's lair in the Hole in the Wall. The cave must still be out there somewhere, under the water.

I smiled to myself and leaned back in my seat to imagine tomorrow.

I began writing a very different version of this story in the 1990s when I was a graduate student at SUNY Binghamton, and I have many people to thank for help along the way as it evolved into the book you now hold in your hands.

First I must thank the people who read early drafts of the work, the writer's group that will always be first in my heart: Susan Campbell Bartoletti, Laura Lee Wren, Clara Gillow Clark, Anna Grossnickle Hines, Gary Hines, Mary Joyce Love, and (God rest her) Norma Grula.

Over the years, the story came to be what it is now with the help of excellent suggestions by Alexandria LaFaye, Hillary Homzie, Han Nolan, Gail Carson Levine, and David Webster. I'm fortunate to have good friends who are also good writers.

The critic who has helped most of all, though, is the editor at Milkweed Editions who acquired the book and pushed me to write beyond better, Ben Barnhart. Thank you, Ben.

Thank you to Eastern Connecticut State University for granting me a sabbatical year during which I did the major revision that led to a contract on the manuscript.

Thank you to the Dougherty Family Foundation for sponsoring the Milkweed Prize for Children's Literature and gifting me with that honor. My heart warms every time I think of it.

I thank my three children, Daisy, Dan, and Livvie, even though they grew up and moved out some time ago, because they inspired many of the ideas in this story. The same goes for all those fifth-graders I used to teach at Wyoming Seminary Lower School in Forty Fort, Pennsylvania.

And finally, I thank my husband, Jeff Meunier. For everything.

LISA ROWE FRAUSTINO is the award-winning author of the novels *Ash*, *Grass and Sky*, and *I Walk in Dread*, and the picture book *The Hickory Chair*. The editor of several anthologies for young adult readers, she teaches children's literature and creative writing at Eastern Connecticut State University and Hollins University. She lives with her husband and four cats in Ashford, Connecticut, and Bowerbank, Maine.

If you enjoyed this book, you'll also want to read these other Milkweed novels.

To order books or for more information, contact Milkweed at (800) 520-6455
or visit our Web site (www.milkweed.org).

Discovering Pig Magic
Julie Crabtree

The Crepe Makers' Bond
Julie Crabtree

Perfect
Natasha Friend

The Keening
A. LaFaye

Milkweed Editions

Founded in 1979, Milkweed Editions is one of the largest independent, nonprofit literary publishers in the United States. Milkweed publishes with the intention of making a humane impact on society, in the belief that good writing can transform the human heart and spirit.

Join Us

Milkweed depends on the generosity of foundations and individuals like you, in addition to the sales of its books. In an increasingly consolidated and bottom-line-driven publishing world, your support allows us to select and publish books on the basis of their literary quality and the depth of their message. Please visit our Web site (www.milkweed.org) or contact us at (800) 520-6455 to learn more about our donor program.

Milkweed Editions, a nonprofit publisher, gratefully acknowledges sustaining support from Emilie and Henry Buchwald; the Patrick and Aimee Butler Foundation; the Dougherty Family Foundation; the Ecolab Foundation; the General Mills Foundation; John and Joanne Gordon; William and Jeanne Grandy; the Jerome Foundation; Robert and Stephanie Karon; the Lerner Foundation; Sally Macut; Sanders and Tasha Marvin; the McKnight Foundation; Mid-Continent Engineering; the Minnesota State Arts Board, through an appropriation by the Minnesota State Legislature, a grant from the Wells Fargo Foundation Minnesota, and a grant from the National Endowment for the Arts; Kelly Morrison and John Willoughby; the National Endowment for the Arts, and the American Reinvestment and Recovery Act; the Navarre Corporation; Ann and Doug Ness; Jörg and Angie Pierach; the RBC Foundation USA; Ellen Sturgis; the Target Foundation; the James R. Thorpe Foundation; the Travelers Foundation; Moira and John Turner; and Edward and Jenny Wahl.

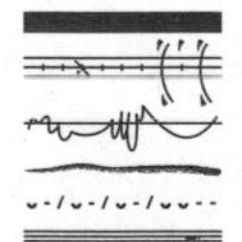

TARGET.

THE McKNIGHT FOUNDATION

Interior design by Connie Kuhnz
Typeset in Rotis Serif
by BookMobile Design and Publishing Services
Printed on acid-free 100% post consumer waste paper
by Friesens Corporation

ENVIRONMENTAL BENEFITS STATEMENT

Milkweed Editions saved the following resources by printing the pages of this book on chlorine free paper made with 100% post-consumer waste.

TREES	WATER	SOLID WASTE	GREENHOUSE GASES
29 FULLY GROWN	**13,364** GALLONS	**811** POUNDS	**2,775** POUNDS

Calculations based on research by Environmental Defense and the Paper Task Force.
Manufactured at Friesens Corporation